W9-CMQ-106

SAN FRANCISCO SERENADE

Other books by Kathleen Fuller:

Santa Fe Sunrise

SAN FRANCISCO SERENADE

•

Kathleen Fuller

AVALON BOOKS
NEW YORK

Published by Thomas Bouregy & Co., Inc.
160 Madison Avenue, New York, NY 10016

Library of Congress Cataloging-in-Publication Data
Fuller, Kathleen.
San Francisco serenade / Kathleen Fuller.
p. cm.
ISBN 0-8034-9747-4 (acid-free paper)
1. San Francisco (Calif.)—Fiction. I. Title.

PS3606.U553S26 2005
813'.6—dc22
2005011567

PRINTED IN THE UNITED STATES OF AMERICA
ON ACID-FREE PAPER
BY HADDON CRAFTSMEN, BLOOMSBURG, PENNSYLVANIA

To Eddie—for everything.

Chapter One

San Francisco 1848

"Oh, Jilly, I'm thrilled you and Roland could make it for the wedding."

Jillian Sanders returned the warm embrace of her childhood friend, Mary Miller, who was now Mary Burns as of three hours ago. Jillian stepped back from Mary, taking in the excited flush of her cheeks and the joy dancing in her smoky brown eyes. In the twenty years she'd known her friend, she'd never seen her so content.

"Was the ride over horrible?" Mary asked.

"Not for me," Jillian said, referring to the long voyage from Australia to California. "Although poor Roland tossed up his accounts more than once."

"Seasickness?"

"He's terribly vulnerable to it."

"Well, then I'm doubly glad you both made it here relatively unscathed. I know it's a far way to travel for a simple wedding."

"There was nothing simple about your wedding, Mary. It was the grandest event I've ever attended. Quite fitting for the wife of one of the most influential men in town."

Mary blushed, her smile growing wider. "So what do you think of America?" Mary linked her arm with Jillian's as they weaved their way around the myriad of guests celebrating the Burns' nuptials.

"Actually it's quite nice," Jillian admitted. "But I'm not certain I'd want to live here." She paused. "Are you certain *you* want to live here?"

"Of course!" Mary laughed. "I'd live anywhere, as long as I'm with my Charles."

"Don't you miss Australia just a tiny bit?"

"I miss you. But you must admit San Francisco isn't all that different from Sydney."

"If you don't count California's upside-down seasons and the odd accents, then I guess it isn't."

"Oh Jilly, you're always so serious."

"Do I really have a choice?"

Mary sobered. "I suppose not. How is your father?"

Jillian sighed. "The illness has taken its toll on both his body and mind."

"I'm sorry."

Jillian caught Mary's empathetic expression and gave her arm a squeeze. "Let's not dwell on the melancholy. After all, we're here to celebrate your marriage!" She smiled, putting her father's malady out of her mind. "Where is your handsome husband, by the way?"

"Over there." Mary pointed to a small gathering of men huddled on the outer corner of the ballroom, talking and laughing. "I do so love that term."

"What term?"

"Husband." She glanced at Jillian slyly. "You should really consider getting your own."

Jillian brushed off her suggestion with one white-gloved hand. "I think not. I have enough trouble keeping track of my brother."

"I believe finding Roland is quite easy," Mary said. "Just locate a bevy of beautiful women and he'll be right in the middle of them."

Jillian looked around the Burns' grand ballroom. Mary's words were proven true a few moments later when she spotted her brother, who was currently the center of attention to a small group of very attractive ladies.

Mary suddenly released Jillian's arm. "Oh, Charles is motioning for me to dance. Do excuse me, Jilly darling. My *husband* awaits." Mary floated across the room on a wave of light pink satin and delighted giggles.

A smile formed on Jillian's lips. Mary and Charles were the perfect couple. Physically they matched well, her dark hair and olive skin tone contrasting with his blond, fair looks. They were complementary in temperament too. And although she missed having Mary live right down the street from her back home in Sydney, she was happy for her friend. Charles Burns owned two of San Francisco's larger banks. Mary's future would be set. Jillian wished she could say the same for herself.

Despite her happiness over Mary's wedding, her trip to San Francisco had a dual purpose. Once the party was over she would return to her room at the Legion Hotel, where she would make notes, conceive plans, and prepare a full report for her father and Martin Holland, the solicitor helping him oversee the company. In two months the family business, Sanders Shipping, would open its first American office. She had tried to get Roland involved in their exciting new venture, but he had only made a halfhearted attempt at strategizing a business plan. That her brother was so disinterested in their company didn't bode well at all for the future of Sanders Shipping.

As if he had somehow known he was the topic of her thoughts, out of the corner of her eye she saw Roland come toward her. By the unevenness of his gait she could tell he was well into his cups. He tipped a rakish grin to a buxom woman as he passed her by. Jillian inwardly groaned.

"Relax, Jilly," her brother smoothly responded as he sidled up beside her. "Stop looking like a woman being forced to walk the plank."

"I wouldn't feel like I was teetering on a plank if I could count on you to behave," she muttered. She released a sigh that bordered on long suffering. Opening her mouth to speak once again, she quickly snapped it shut, thinking better of it. It would be a pointless exercise, really. Her younger sibling had never been one for listening to reason.

Roland glanced at her, flashing the mischievous glint in his eye that often had most of Sydney's eligible young ladies—and a few uneligible ones—turning into fawning fools. "Jilly, I believe you could wilt a bouquet of roses with that sour expression on your face. You're best friend just got married. Why can't you just enjoy yourself for once?"

"Because I know what you're capable of." Her voice dripped with caustic annoyance. "Especially when you've been drinking."

"If that remark had come from any woman other than my sister, I would be flattered. Instead I'm just insulted."

Jillian touched the cameo pin at her throat, resisting the urge to reach for her handkerchief and dab at her brow, which more than likely shined with perspiration. It was winter back in Australia, and she had dressed for a chilly August night. She hadn't anticipated how warm it was during the summertime in San Francisco.

Her brother, on the other hand, looked as cool as an ocean breeze, a lock of his reddish blond hair falling over one eyebrow, his charming smile firmly in place.

Good grief, he was irritating.

Ignoring the interested glances directed at Roland by several of the ladies in attendance, Jillian canvassed the room. Superb didn't begin to describe it, with its vast and ornately carved high ceiling, gilt wall mirrors and green velvet drapes trimmed with gold fringe. The polished floor gleamed in the flickering light of numerous candles and the mellow glow of gas lighting.

Across the room, she could hear the soft notes of the string quartet, and the dull knock of dancing footsteps on the ballroom floor.

"Champagne?" A smartly attired servant held a silver tray before her, laden with several stemmed glasses. Pale liquid sparkled in each one.

"Absolutely." Roland eagerly snatched up a glass.

Jillian cut her brother a look of reproach. "No thank you," she said, declining the beverage. The balding servant nodded slightly and left.

Roland took a long swallow from his glass. He tipped it toward her. "Ah, champagne," he said, a satisfied look forming on his face. "A rip snorter of a drink, wouldn't you say?"

"No, I wouldn't."

He chuckled. "Of course you wouldn't. How could I forget the ever proper, ever *uptight* Jillian Sanders would never use such a common phrase as 'rip snorter.' "

"Oh, please," Jillian said. "I am *not* uptight. And I'm warning you, if you get off your face tonight—"

"My point exactly." He drained his drink. "Not to worry, I won't embarrass you by getting drunk. *This time*," he added with a wink. "I promise I'll drink in moderation."

"See that you do. You know the last thing

Father needs is for you to besmirch the family name before we even open for business."

His good humor dissipated. "Oh yes, Father can't have that, can he?" he said snidely.

"Roland, don't start—"

"You're worse than a mother hen, you know that? Now, if you don't mind, I think I'll mix and mingle. You never know what kind of 'business contacts' one might meet at a soiree like this." With that he walked away, melting into the crush of people gathering in the grand ballroom.

"Don't you dare leave me . . . alone." She pressed her lips together as she watched him disappear. *I would have been better off coming here by myself*. Of course that idea was out of the question—she couldn't show up at such an event without an escort, even at her best friend's wedding.

"Oh, if I were a man," she grumbled to herself, "I could run the business myself." But that was impossible. Although her father had taught her everything about the company and had trained her in handling the accounts, she had little hope for using her skills in any permanent capacity. In fact, she doubted she'd ever return to America once her father was well enough to make the journey here. No, like all women her age, soon she would be married and have children, spending the rest of her life changing dirty pants and wiping snotty noses back home in Sydney.

The thought made her stomach churn.

Forcing away the distasteful thread weaving in her mind, she surveyed the people around her, making mental notes along the way. Truth be told, she hated parties like this. She wasn't skilled at small talk, and she certainly couldn't elbow her way in on any business conversations the men were having. She'd have to concentrate more on peripheral details. The musicians were very good, she had to admit. She'd always enjoyed a good quartet. And the women were dressed fashionably well. The men were gathered in small clumps on the perimeter of the room, presumably talking money, politics, and the attributes of high quality cigars.

Then her perusal stopped suddenly. Standing near the musicians she saw three gentlemen, two of them with their backs to her. But the one facing her, his coal black hair combed back from his handsome, strong face, made her heart flutter in her chest. It was an odd sensation, one she had never experienced before. She simply couldn't keep her eyes off him.

The man was steeped in conversation, but suddenly, as if sensing her inspection, he looked directly at her. And smiled.

Her face suffusing with heat, she turned away. She felt like a child caught with her hand in the treat jar. Still, she couldn't help the warm emotion that flooded her at the sight of his smile, his dark mustache accenting the perfect shape of his lips.

She gave her head a shake. What was she doing, becoming besotted with a mere stranger? Becoming besotted period? There was no reason for such ridiculousness. Entertaining foolish thoughts and feelings about an unknown man served no purpose. Closing her eyes, she put his image out of her mind and continued her circumspect study of the people around her. She was here to support her friend and help her father, nothing more.

But it took every bit of inner strength not to seek out the striking gentleman again.

"Ethan. Ethan? Are you even listening to me?"

Ethan Vincent forced himself to pay attention to the conversation. It was difficult, since the drone of his father's voice continually caused his attention to wander.

"As I was saying, it seems we're in for some competition soon." Vincent tucked his hand into a gap between the strained buttons on his striped waistcoat. "Not that I'm worried about that.

Competition is good for the heart and soul. Besides, I'll crush him before he has a chance to get his first ship out of port."

Herman Faraday, the Boston businessman who had joined them in conversation, chuckled. "I knew there was a reason I liked you, Vincent. I think further discussion about a partnership is well overdue. Perhaps you and I can retire to the library and continue this conversation?"

"Anything you have to say can be said in front of my son. He has just as much invested in Vincent and Son Shipping as I do."

"Very well." Faraday began talking, but it wasn't long before Ethan tuned them out, looking for the beautiful woman who had caught his eye a few minutes ago.

She seemed to have vanished into the crowd, which was easy to do considering the number of guests invited to the wedding celebration. Although he didn't know the Burnses that well, he had to admit they threw a fine party.

"I shall be returning to Boston in the next couple of days," Faraday said, his voice barely registering in Ethan's ears. "From there, my daughter Melanie and I are planning to move to Santa Fe."

"Santa Fe?" Harold remarked, his bushy brows rising in surprise. "Why would you want to live there?"

"There are business opportunities galore as a result of the Santa Fe trail. I'm hoping to capitalize on some of them."

"Just as you hope to capitalize on a business opportunity with me."

"Precisely. Perhaps the future will be beneficial to us both."

Suddenly Ethan saw her again. She was standing alone, looking rather bemused. He had yet to see anyone approach her for a dance, which he found odd considering how beautiful she was. Her strawberry blond curls cascaded from underneath a small light blue hat decorated with a simple jeweled pin. She was unlike anyone he'd ever seen, lovely and graceful, and with a determined set to her chin. A brilliant ruby among a sea of pearls. She turned and started walking away again.

He wouldn't lose her this time.

"Would you both excuse me," he said quickly, knowing he was being rude to his father and Herman Faraday but leaving them anyway. With lengthened strides he walked toward the young woman.

Relief washed over him as he saw her pause and turn in his direction. Surprise registered in her eyes as he approached, but she didn't look away.

The quartet began another lively tune. Ethan grasped the opportunity. "May I have this dance?" he asked, extending his hand.

"I don't think so."

Her refusal surprised him, but he wouldn't be deterred. "Are you sure? Because it looked to me as if you were enjoying the music."

"I am," she admitted in a somewhat reluctant tone.

"Then I think a dance is in order. Unless the reason you're turning me down is because you don't dance."

"Of course I dance," she said, an edge creeping into her voice. "It's just that . . . well, I just . . ."

"You just . . . what?"

"I just don't want to, that's all."

"The way you're tapping your foot in time with the music tells me different." He watched as she glanced down at her feet and immediately stilled her movements. Then he moved beside her.

For the next few minutes they stood side by side, watching the other couples as they swirled around the ballroom floor. Ethan started whistling to the music, his hands clasped behind him.

"You don't have to remain here," she said after a lengthy silence. "I'm sure there are plenty of other women who would be more than happy to dance with you."

"Perhaps, but none of them would be quite as intriguing as you." He turned and faced her. "Or as beautiful."

Her face flushed as she shyly looked away. "You flatter me, sir."

"Not flattery, just honesty." Before she had a chance to protest again he grasped her hand and deftly guided her to the floor.

"Sir!" she said, stiffening in his arms. "Are you in the habit of whisking women away against their will?"

"No," he answered truthfully. "But you're the exception to the rule."

Chapter Two

If Ethan had thought her beautiful from afar, she was more exquisite up close. Her eyes were bluer than the sea itself, with dark blond eyelashes fringing around them. Her skin was slightly darker than the pampered ladies he was used to being around, suggesting she spent a good amount of time in the sun. Her accent was unusual, reminding him a bit of Charles' bride's accent.

Seamlessly they circled the expanse of the floor. Not only was she lovely, but she was also an incredible dancer. Once she relaxed, that is. She seemed wound up tighter than a spool of thread.

Surely she was here visiting someone, because he hadn't seen her before. If he had, he wouldn't have forgotten her. Quite the opposite—he would have remembered her for the rest of his life.

"Where are you from?" he asked, eager to know more about her.

"Australia." Her answer was clipped.

She was so guarded, as if she held a multitude of secrets behind those luminous eyes. He had always been drawn to mysterious women, and he wanted to know what she kept so carefully veiled. "Let me guess—you're a guest of the bride's."

She nodded. "We are childhood friends from Sydney."

"Remind me to compliment Mary on the company she keeps. Oh, is that the barest hint of a smile I see?"

Her smile grew. "Are you always this impertinent, Mr . . . ?"

"Ethan, if you please. And no, to be honest, I'm very shy around the ladies."

"I find that hard to believe." She tilted her body to the side a bit, avoiding a collision with an overly enthusiastic dancer. "You seem to be the type of man who regularly sweeps damsels off their feet."

"Actually I spend more time tripping over them." As if on cue, his foot pressed against the tip of her shoe. "Sorry. See what I mean?"

"I think you're a splendid dancer."

He grinned. "Say that again."

Bewilderment crossed her features. "Say what again?"

"That I'm splendid."

She chuckled. "I said you're a splendid *dancer*. Whether you're anything more remains to be seen."

Her icy façade was melting right before his eyes, and it warmed his heart. "It's nice to see you enjoying the party."

"I'm not, really." Her eyes suddenly grew wide. "I probably shouldn't have said that."

"Probably not. But I sympathize with you." He gestured to the partygoers with a tilt of his head. "I only come to these things because it's expected of me."

The last strains of music suddenly faded into silence, followed by the muted clapping of many white-gloved hands.

"Thank you for the dance, Ethan."

Although proper decorum would be to tell her his last name, for some reason he held back. He didn't want her to refer to him as Mr. Vincent. It was too cold and impersonal. The last thing he wanted to be with this woman was impersonal. "And your name is?"

She hesitated for a moment, as if debating on whether to answer him. "Jillian," she finally responded. "Jillian."

Tucking her hand in the crook of his arm and covering it with his own, he asked, "Can I interest you in a drink, Jillian?"

Glancing down at her hand snugly ensconced in his grasp, she frowned. When he felt her fingers move ever so slightly, he knew she was going to refuse his request.

He wasn't about to let her do that.

Jillian stared at her hand. She could feel the warmth of Ethan's palm through her glove. He had strong hands. She had noticed that when he first brought her out on the dance floor. He was also too bold and too familiar. Not to mention too handsome and too charming for his own good.

She sighed inwardly. She didn't need any personal entanglements, especially not with a man this hard to resist. Yet she couldn't pull herself away from him. Following his lead, she'd given him only her first name, something she'd never offered a gentleman before. Their dance had been beyond lovely, and she found herself wishing it would continue forever. But like the final notes of a waltz, it had to come to an end.

"Let's forget the drink," Ethan said, interrupting her thoughts. "We can go out onto the balcony instead. Escape the party for a few minutes."

That sounded wonderful. And too tempting to refuse. "For a few minutes," she found herself saying. "A few minutes *only*," she clarified.

"That's all I'm asking."

They walked to a huge set of French doors. Grasping the brass handle, Ethan opened them, leading her out to the balcony. Jillian followed, then stopped. "There's no one else out here," she said, surprised.

"Don't worry," Ethan said, taking her by the arm again. "I promise I'll behave."

Despite the mischief in his eyes, she knew in her heart she could trust him.

Stepping toward the wrought iron railing that bordered the stone balcony, she breathed in the familiar scent of the ocean. Immediately she relaxed, happy for the reprieve from the cloying wedding reception.

He came up beside her, leaning over the railing and placing his forearms on top of it. "Nothing like the salty air to ease the tension away," he said, putting voice to how she was feeling.

It was as if he could read her thoughts, sense

her emotions. Very odd, considering they'd only known each other for a brief time. Then again this evening had taken an ethereal turn ever since she'd met him. And being in his presence seemed to make all her looming problems fade into the background.

They both turned to each other at the same time. Her eyes locked with his for a brief moment, then her gaze searched his face. She had this incredible urge to memorize every detail of it, from his hooded gray eyes to his neatly trimmed mustache to his strong jawline. He was by far the most handsome man she'd ever encountered.

The joviality in his eyes dimmed, changing to a smoky color. His ever ready smile faded as his expression grew in intensity, causing warmth to spread through her entire body.

"Jillian," he said, his voice as gentle and as soft as a whisper. "I know I promised to be a gentleman . . ." He leaned in closer.

Her throat became dry, and she swallowed, even as she met his forward movement with her own.

"But . . ." his mouth hovered above hers, "I'm finding it more difficult than I thought."

She licked her trembling lips. "Then . . . don't think."

His kiss was sweet and innocent, but it stirred

a fire in her nevertheless. His lips touched hers for the briefest of moments before he pulled away.

Suddenly the doors flew open, causing them to jump apart. Jillian's hand flew unbidden to her heated face as her brother rushed toward her.

"Jillian, I've been looking everywhere for you." His face was ashen, his eyes panicked. Fear jumped inside her—she had never seen Roland like this before.

"It's Father," he said. "The news isn't good. We must hurry back to Sydney. Now."

His lips still tingling from their kiss, Ethan watched as Jillian was escorted away by the young man. The color had drained from her face upon receiving the news about her father. Immediately he followed them into the milling crowd, his worry for her intensifying with each step. They were nearing the exit when a woman's shrill voice filled his ears.

"Yoo-hoo! Mr. Vincent!" Henrietta Mulberry daintily waved a white handkerchief in the air as she bustled her way to him, her reluctant daughter Hannah lagging directly behind. "May we have a word?"

Ethan grimaced. It was never "a word" with Mrs. Mulberry, it was many words. Many, many,

many words. "Not now," he said tersely as Jillian headed out the door.

If Mrs. Mulberry was put off by his curt response, she didn't show it. Instead she placed her rotund body in between him and the ballroom exit. "Hannah, do hurry up!" she hissed at her daughter, who was still moving like an ancient turtle.

Hannah quickened her steps and came up beside her mother, then immediately averted her gaze, her cheeks flushing. The poor girl had always been painfully shy, something her obtuse mother never seemed to realize.

"As I was saying," Henrietta continued. "Mr. Mulberry and I would love to commission you to paint our Hannah's portrait. I was thinking about an outdoor background. Our garden has bloomed lush and full this year. The roses and delphinium will be a lovely contrast to Hannah's dark hair and peachy skin, don't you think Mr. Vincent?"

Ethan craned his neck and tried to look around Henrietta. "I don't do portraiture—"

"Oh, nonsense, of course you do. You're an artist, aren't you?"

"It's only a hobby, really—"

"Your mother certainly sings your praises. She says you can draw, paint, and sculpt anything. Although your father has never mentioned a word about it, oddly enough. Anyway, you'll be well compensated for your work, I can assure you. Nothing but the best for our darling Hannah."

"Mother," Hannah whispered harshly, the skin of her scalp where her hair was parted turning bright pink.

"So you'll come by tomorrow and do some preliminary sketches?" Henrietta asked. "About six or so?"

He tried to step around her, but with each movement he made, she matched it. He was dangerously close to shoving the annoying woman out of the way. "Mrs. Mulberry, if we could discuss this later—"

"Ethan. A word."

Ethan clenched his jaw at the sound of his father's voice behind him. He was trapped between the two of them. There was no escape now.

"Yes, Father?" he said through gritted teeth.

"Mrs. Mulberry, so nice to see you," Harold said, taking the time to be polite despite his obvious impatience, the fact that the Mulberrys were among the richest citizens in San Francisco being the reason why. "May I speak to my son for a moment?"

"Certainly. But don't forget about tomorrow, Ethan," she added. "Hannah will be waiting."

As the women turned and left, Harold regarded his son. "What was all that about?"

"Nothing," Ethan replied, eyeing the ballroom door. Maybe there was still time to find Jillian if he quickly got rid of his father. He couldn't just let her disappear like that. Not after the magical moments they'd shared. He shifted back and forth on his feet, stealing backward glances at the door. "You wanted to speak to me?"

"Faraday and I have been talking," he said. "He has a proposition, one that will make both our families very rich indeed."

"Families?"

Vincent nodded. "Congratulations. You're officially betrothed."

"What?" Ethan's mouth fell open, shock replaced his impatience. "Betrothed? To whom?"

"Melanie Faraday, of course. By this time next year you'll be a married man."

Chapter Three

San Francisco, 1849
One year later

Ethan sketched a few finishing touches to the ship design laid out on the huge desk in front of him. During the past couple months he had been studying and working on the drawing of a sleeker, more powerful clipper ship.

Folding the piece of paper into a small square, he tucked it in his pocket and rose from his father's desk. A desk he would someday call his own, as the future head of Vincent and Son. It was a thought that never failed to cause mixed feelings inside him. He had no head for books, and the day-to-day running of the business hardly interested him. It never had, much to his father's chagrin.

Ethan pushed up his worn, chambray sleeves. Dressed in an old shirt and even older trousers, he looked as if he belonged on the docks as opposed to an ornate office. He'd rather be on the docks too.

He loved the ships. Since he was a child running around the deck of his father's first small craft, he'd always been fascinated with them. Their power, their beauty, their speed. He knew every square inch of each vessel, from the top of the tallest sail to the last plank beneath the galley. Even now he enjoyed spending time on the docks, exploring the ships, mingling with the crew, learning all he could about sailing and life on the high seas.

Crossing the expansive room, he walked over to the open window and stared out at the sea. Foamy waves lopped at the sides of several ships, two of which were readying to depart the port. He breathed in the salty tang of the air and listened to the sharp squawks of circling seagulls. His fingers itched to hold charcoal and paper so he could sketch the peaceful scene.

An image flitted across his mind, triggered by the memory of another time spent on a balcony overlooking the sea. Golden red hair. Warm, strawberry tinted lips. A soft voice with a charming accent . . .

"I didn't spend most of my life building Vincent & Son so you could daydream it away."

Ethan's head snapped around at the sound of his father's voice. The beautiful vision flew out of his mind, and he whirled around to see Harold Vincent standing in the doorway.

"I'm not daydreaming," Ethan said, ignoring the fact he'd told a half-truth. "Merely thinking."

Harold entered the room and went behind the desk. He squeezed his sizable frame into the chair. "Unless you're thinking about profit, you're daydreaming." He looked at the ledgers and frowned.

"Profits are fine."

"How would you know? When was the last time you looked at a ledger? Or sat in on a meeting with an associate? Sometimes I wonder if you care about this company at all."

Ethan cringed. The name may have read Vincent and Son over the warehouse, but the partnership was hardly equal. He doubted it ever would be. "Of course I care. In fact, there's something I want to show you. I've been working on a sketch—"

"Don't tell me. You've designed another clipper ship."

"Yes, I have," Ethan replied, excitement creeping into his voice. "I think I've come up with a way to make our ships slightly faster while on their routes." He started to retrieve the drawing when his father held up his hand dismissively.

"Our ships are fine the way they are. They're the best in all of San Francisco."

"But with the improvements—"

"Ethan, the company neither has the time, nor the money to build new ships. Not when the ones we have are in perfect working order." He sighed. "How can I make you understand, son? The secret to success lies in paying attention to profit margins, cultivating new merchants, and keeping a keen eye on the competition, not wasting time scratching pictures on a piece of paper."

Ethan left his sketch in his pocket.

Harold retrieved a cigar from the breast pocket of his jacket. "Of course, if you had married that Faraday woman, profits might never have been an issue again. You could have at least made that contribution to the company."

Walking over to the opposite side of the desk, Ethan sat down, feeling insignificant in the shadow of the large piece of furniture and the imposing man behind it. Why was it he could feel confident in anyone else's presence except his father's?

The man never failed to make him feel like a little boy still wet behind the ears.

"Miss Faraday was in love with someone else," Ethan said, explaining the situation for what seemed like the hundredth time.

Although months had passed since Ethan had traveled to New Mexico territory with Mr. Faraday to track down the man's wayward daughter, Harold never failed to let Ethan know how disappointed he was that the engagement had been terminated.

"What does love have to do with anything?" Harold scoffed. "She was betrothed to *you*."

"But not of her own free will. Would you have me marry a woman whose heart belonged to someone else?"

Harold paused. Ethan gave him a small bit of credit for that. But in the end his father said exactly what Ethan had expected him to say. "For the sake of the business and the security of your future, yes. I would have."

"That would have hardly been fair. To either one of us."

"Nothing's fair in life. The sooner you learn that, the better." His gray eyes hardened as he snipped the end of his cigar. "I'm sure you two would have had an amiable relationship."

"Amiable, yes." From his brief encounter with

Melanie Faraday he had discerned she was a nice girl. A bit impulsive, but nice. He fully believed she'd have made a suitable wife.

But he wasn't looking for someone "suitable." And Melanie's heart wasn't the only one that had been captured by someone else. His own had been stolen by a beautiful, mysterious woman named Jillian. But he knew he'd never see her again.

Despite his father's edict that he be betrothed to Melanie, Ethan had gone straight to Mary Burns to find out when Jillian had left, and if she'd ever return. Mary's response had nearly broken his heart. Now an ocean divided him and Jillian, one that would be almost impossible to cross, unless he stowed away on a ship headed for Australia, which was completely out of the question.

Knowing she was out of his life forever, he pragmatically agreed to his father's arranged engagement. He could at least see the practicality of it. And whatever he had to lose had already been lost.

But despite it all, Jillian was never far from his thoughts. He wondered if she ever would be.

The scent of sulfur permeated the air as Harold struck a match and brought it to the tip of the cigar. "Ah, well, it's a moot point anyway," he said, drawing in a few puffs. "I hear Ms. Faraday is already wed and has moved on to San Antonio. Why anyone would want to live in Texas is a mystery to me." He exhaled a perfect smoke ring. "Still, I hate to see another business opportunity lost."

Scrubbing his hand over his clean shaven face, Ethan met his father's disappointed gaze, knowing the man still blamed Ethan for ruining what should have been a sure thing.

Harold stuck the cigar between his teeth and abruptly stood up. "I'm going to meet with the constable this morning regarding that scoundrel, Watkins. I want to make sure he's locked up for good. I will personally throw away the key myself."

Ethan nodded, glad to see the subject of Melanie Faraday dropped, hopefully for good. The company's former solicitor had hired Dell Watkins as an overseer a year ago, but this had proved disastrous. The man had stolen hundreds of dollars from the company by embezzling it before they had uncovered his treachery last month. Watkins and the solicitor were both in the San Francisco jail.

"The *Edwina Columbia* is set to sail in two hours," Harold continued, a scowl deepening the lines on his face. "Go down to the ship and double-check the master list. I don't want any illicit cargo smuggled on board."

Ethan nodded, despite knowing the captain of the ship had already accomplished that exact same task. But after the debacle with Watkins he didn't blame his father for wanting to be extra careful.

Harold removed his cigar from between his teeth. "One more thing. Seems your mother and I have been invited to one of those boring musicales next week. The Prestons are putting this one on, I believe. And since I'd rather stick hot pokers in my eyeballs than be endlessly serenaded by a bunch of dullards, I told her you would go in my stead."

"Consider it done." Even though he detested musicales as much as his father, he didn't want to disappoint his mother, who enjoyed them very much.

"Good. At least I can depend on you for something." Placing his hat on his balding pate, he touched the rim. "Don't forget about the list."

"I won't."

"We can't afford another problem like Watkins. I'm counting on you, Ethan."

Ethan inhaled an uncertain breath. *I know you are.*

* * *

"Roland." Jillian walked over to her brother, who was leaning against the huge mast in the middle of the *Clarabella*. "The ship moored over thirty minutes ago."

Roland shot her a sickly look and clutched his stomach, which had been emptied several times over the course of their voyage from Sydney. "Bloody seasickness," he moaned.

"I'm sorry," she said, taking in his pasty complexion. "It was really awful, wasn't it?"

"Horrible." He let out a faint chuckle as he reached for Jillian's arm, gripping it as if his fingers were a vise.

"I can hardly see the humor in this, Roland." She led him down the wooden plank that straddled the thin strip of water separating the dock from the ship.

"Not humor, darling Jilly. Irony. Bitter, bitter irony. The son of a shipping magnate, reduced to a puking mess the moment he steps foot on a ship." He looked at her. "If only I had your constitution."

Gingerly they made their way to the dock. Once reaching steady land, he straightened slightly. "Thank the Lord," he mumbled. "We're finally here."

Jillian inhaled deeply. Yes, they were. After an interminably long voyage they had set foot in San Francisco. Their new home. Tears burned her eyes. She blinked them back. It had been six months since her father had died and the pain was still raw.

"Jilly?" Roland halted. "Are you all right?"

"Yes," she said, digging deep for inner strength. She knew Roland was already apprehensive about his new role as head of the American division of the company. But it had been their father's last request, and he had had no choice but to accept the position, even though he knew almost nothing about the company. She had little choice either but to accept their father's edict, and to be there for her brother and for the company. They didn't leave their home and everything behind to fail. She would make sure they wouldn't.

As they walked along the dock, she could hear the sounds of wood creaking and men shouting. She could smell the scent of sea air and pungent fish. She could see the tall, magnificent ships that lined the port and the sailors bustling about, preparing their vessels for departure. These were things she was used to. Suddenly she felt a little better.

"Oh no," Roland groaned, letting go of her arm and clasping his gut. "And I'm not even on the boat anymore." Dashing over to the side of the dock, he retched into the brackish water.

Jillian made no move to follow him, knowing

from experience that he preferred to suffer alone. That is if one considered throwing up on a crowded pier as being alone. She turned away, desperate for something to distract her until he was finished.

She spied a grand ship teeming with activity. Squinting, she read the name on the side: *Edwina Columbia*. A worthy vessel indeed. She continued to inspect the ship from a distance. But her scrutiny stopped at the sight of two men approaching the craft.

She peered surreptitiously at them. One was short and squat with a well-worn cap perched jauntily on his head. He was obviously a captain. But he wasn't the one that captured her attention. It was his tall, broad shouldered cohort. A sense of familiarity stole over her, causing her palms to perspire underneath her white cotton gloves. *No. It couldn't be . . .*

He had infiltrated her dreams since that night many months ago, when she and Roland had last been in San Francisco. When Ethan had swept her onto the dance floor and charmed her to her core. She could still remember the feel of his hand at her back, the warmth in his gray eyes as they had danced together. The light pressure of his lips when they had kissed. Then she had gotten the terrible news about her father . . .

For the past year she had tried to ignore her

thoughts about him, tried to pretend that their time together had been but silly moments of fancy best put to rest in the vault of her memory. But she couldn't. He was indelibly marked in her mind. And her heart.

But was this the same man? By his style of dress he looked more like a roughened sailor than a gentleman at ease at a fancy party.

"Jilly, I beg of you," Roland said weakly, coming up behind her. "We must get to the hotel as soon as possible. Casting up accounts on the public dock is not exactly how I wanted to make an impression."

Giving her head a small shake, she tore her gaze from the subject of her musings. "Of course, Roland. We shall go right away."

"Thank you." He sighed. "A nice, comfortable bed is what I need right now."

Jillian guided him down the docks. As she neared the two men they turned and walked toward the ship, their backs to her. Disappointed at not having a closer look, she resigned herself to what was most likely the truth—this man was not the one who made her heart race and her pulse pound.

Still, she held a tiny fragment of hope that someday, somewhere, she and Ethan would meet again.

Chapter Four

"Mary, really, I haven't time for this."

"Jilly, there's always time for fun." Mary tugged on a pair of white satin elbow-length gloves. "You've done nothing but lock yourself up in that office for hours. Even Roland isn't as obsessed as you are, and he's the head of the company."

Hardly. Roland had managed to make himself scarce for most of the past week, while Jillian had been busy getting Sanders Shipping off the ground. Her eyes were blurry from staring at reams of facts and figures, cargo lists, and reports on the other shipping companies in the area. She gave up on enlisting her brother's help after only two days. She just didn't have the mental and emotional energy to argue with him.

No, there wasn't a doubt in Jillian's mind that Roland had found plenty of entertainment outside the walls of Sanders Shipping.

"You've always liked music," Mary continued, checking her flawless complexion in the gilded looking glass that stood in the corner of her dressing room. She had convinced Jillian to come over a couple hours earlier, and they were getting ready for the Prestons' musicale together, just as they had done for so many events as young girls back in Sydney. "And I know you'll simply adore the Golden Quartet. They were the group that played at my wedding."

"They were excellent."

"See? I can tell you're intrigued already."

"I didn't say I was intrigued. I just agreed with your assessment of the musicians."

"Jillian, please." Mary came up to her and placed her hands on her friend's shoulders. "You're driving yourself too hard. You barely had a chance to mourn for your father. I know you take your role as Roland's assistant very seriously, but the company won't fail if you're not there every minute."

It took all Jillian had not to contradict Mary's words. To confess that yes, the company *would* fail if she weren't there to keep it running. The good Lord knew Roland wasn't interested in the job. His only concern was spending the profits.

But she couldn't let anyone else know that. If word got out that she ran the day-to-day business of the company, Sanders Shipping would sink faster than a rowboat with half the bottom missing. Her father might have been the son of an exiled criminal, yet he had built a successful business through hard work and dedication. She wouldn't let anything ruin that.

A knock sounded at the bedroom door. "Mary, darling? Are you ready?"

"Yes, Charles." She looked at Jillian and smiled. "I believe we are. We'll meet you downstairs."

"I suppose there's no way I can get out of this?" Jillian said, resigned.

"No." Mary brushed some invisible lint off of Jillian's sea green gown. Grasping Jillian's hand, she led her to the door. "You're going to have a grand time tonight, despite your best attempts not to."

"Ethan, you are such a dear for escorting me to this party." Bessie Vincent flashed a beaming smile at her son as they entered the Prestons' drawing room.

"My pleasure, Mother. It isn't often I have a beautiful woman on my arm."

"Flattery will get you everywhere," his mother laughed. "You've known that since you were a child."

"Ah, my secret is out." Ethan grinned down at his mother, who looked resplendent in her dark blue gown.

"It was hardly a secret, darling." Her gaiety dimmed. "If only your father would express more of an interest in these types of things like he used to." As if she'd mentally shaken off an unpleasant thought, she turned to Ethan, her rosy cheeks plumping as she smiled. "I believe I see Mrs. Thorsten across the room." She lifted one gloved hand in a tiny wave. "I'll return shortly. Do try to find us a seat near the front."

Ethan nodded as she turned and walked away. Standing by the entrance, he scanned the room, recognizing a few faces. Mr. and Mrs. Westington occupied the corner of the room, looking as sullen as usual. The buxom widow Myers was flirting with a man at least twenty years her junior, her usual target age. Charles Burns, who had just entered the room with his wife Mary on one arm and another woman loosely clasping the other.

His heart instantly leaped to his throat as his gaze locked on the second woman. *Jillian*. He could scarcely believe she was here.

He watched as she released Charles' arm and let the couple walk a few steps ahead of her. She was as beautiful as he remembered, the muted green color of her dress drawing out the shiny hue of her reddish blond hair, her grace and regal carriage still stunning. He wanted to approach her, but his feet were frozen in place.

He couldn't stop looking at her, drinking his fill of her with his eyes. Then his excitement dimmed slightly. He could see she was troubled. She looked as if she carried the weight of the world on her slim shoulders.

"Ethan dear, I have found us the perfect seat. Ethan?"

"What?" He turned to his mother, who was standing next to him. He hadn't heard her approach. "Sorry. I was thinking about something else."

"That's all right," she said, patting his arm. "You're entitled to daydream. It's good for the soul. As I was saying, Charles and Mary Burns were nice enough to reserve seats for us. They're such a lovely young couple, don't you think?"

"They certainly are." His good humor returned. If he were seated by the Burnses, more than likely he would be near Jillian. He wouldn't have to seek her out—Mary had unknowingly brought her practically straight to him.

Ethan hastily escorted his mother to the front of the room, in the fourth row where the Burnses were already seated. Bessie moved to sit on the opposite side of Charles, and Ethan started to follow her.

His gaze immediately converged on Jillian. Relief washed over him as he saw the chair to the left of hers was empty. As the lights began to dim, he quickly sat down in the seat.

He could barely make out her features in the residual candlelight. The flickering shadows danced charmingly across her profile as the quartet began playing the opening strains of their first tune. He leaned closer to her. "Lovely gathering," he said. "The musicians are quite good."

"Yes," she said, not looking at him, seemingly preoccupied with something else.

Oh, she smelled wonderful, like peaches in summertime. He fought the urge to make a complete fool of himself by closing his eyes and inhaling her scent. "They are the finest in San Francisco," he managed to say.

"I'll take your word for it." Her lips barely moved during her soft reply.

"Shhhhh." The elderly Miss Bradstone, who was seated directly in front of them, swiveled around in her chair, her mouth pursed in her usual sour expression. "Be quiet!"

"Yes ma'am," Ethan said contritely, irritated that with one withering look the old biddy could make him feel as if he were back in grammar school. Considering Miss Bradstone had once been his teacher and he had already been on the receiving end of countless withering looks, he shouldn't have been surprised.

But his irritation didn't merely extend to the cranky Miss Bradstone. Why was Jillian ignoring him? Had she completely forgotten about their encounter during her absence?

For the next few minutes they sat and listened to the music. Ethan tried to concentrate on the musicianship, but he found himself stealing sideways glances at every opportunity, willing her to look at him again. Initially she seemed impatient with the program, as if she were ready for it to end. But soon he noticed her relaxing, seemingly enjoying the lilting song that filtered through the air.

Then the performance was over. The lights were brightened while everyone clapped. Turning to his right, he met her eyes, able to see her clearly the first time that evening.

"That was wonderful," she said, her voice soft and breathy as she turned to look at him.

"Yes," he replied. "It was . . . wonderful."

She tilted her head to the side, and recognition

finally dawned. Her eyes widened, and the fan she'd been holding dropped to the floor. "Oh my goodness, it's *you!*"

Jillian's heart jolted. *Ethan.* The man from her dreams had been sitting next to her the whole time and she hadn't realized it. She'd been so steeped in her own worries about the company and Roland that she hadn't given him much thought when he sat down next to her, thinking he was just another nameless stranger.

"Oh, Jilly, I see you've met Ethan." Mary suddenly appeared beside her. She and Charles were practically joined at the hip. "Jilly is one of my closest childhood friends from Sydney."

"Actually, we've met before," Ethan said, a smile forming on his lips.

Jillian didn't reply. Instead she continued to stare at the handsome man in front of her. He had changed since those months long ago. Gone was the mustache and his hair brushed past his collar, a little longer than the current style. It was neatly slicked back, wonderfully framing his strong features.

"You have! How wonderful." Mary paused for a moment, her eyes flitting from Ethan to Jillian then back to Ethan again. "Charles and I were about to catch a breath of fresh air out in the garden," Mary said. "It's a beautiful night. Would you care to join us, Mr. Vincent?"

Vincent. The name sounded familiar, but Jillian couldn't recall why.

"I'd be delighted to," Ethan replied, then looked at Jillian. "That is if Jillian will accompany us as well."

"Well, I—"

"Of course she will!" Mary beamed at her friend. "I had intended to show her the grand view from the Prestons' garden anyway."

"But its dark outside," Jillian pointed out.

Mary looked unnerved, but only for a moment. "I meant the grand view of the garden itself," she said with a slightly forced chuckle. "The Prestons' garden is well known in San Francisco for its, uh, grand view. Right Charles?"

"Right," Charles returned, after his wife jabbed a very noticeable elbow in his ribs.

Jillian looked at Ethan, assuming he was as uncomfortable as she was with Mary's blatant attempts at pushing them together. But from the amused gleam in his silvery eyes he looked anything but disconcerted. In fact, he seemed to be enjoying himself.

"I'll tell you what," Ethan said to Mary. "I would be honored to show Jillian the Prestons' garden. I'm sure she's never seen one like it."

"Perfect." Mary turned to her husband. "Charles, I'm suddenly parched. Why don't we go by the refreshment table and get ourselves a drink before we go outside?" She threaded her arm through his and guided him away from Jillian and Ethan. "Enjoy the view," she said, casting Jillian a knowing look.

Mortified, Jillian turned to Ethan. "I'm sorry about that. Really, we don't have to do anything. If you'd prefer to part company, I'd understand completely. Sometimes Mary can be less than subtle."

"I can tell. But in this case I'm glad she is," he smiled. "It's wonderful to see you again, Jillian."

"You too," she responded softly.

He extended his arm. "Shall we go? We wouldn't want to disappoint your friend, would we?"

Jillian dropped her gaze to his extended arm. She should leave. She had a mile-long list of things to do tomorrow, and it was growing late. How could she expect the company to survive if she spent her nights indulged in frivolity?

Then she looked up at Ethan, his eyes silently encouraging her to go with him. The warmth she saw there infiltrated her being, and it was irresistible. It made her want to forget about business, forget about her problems with Roland, and forget about the emptiness she'd felt in her heart since her father died. Shoving it all away, she accepted Ethan's invitation. "Why yes, Ethan, I would love to accompany you."

"Right this way."

Her hand firmly resting on the inside of his crooked elbow, Jillian allowed him to lead her through the crush of people to the outside of the Preston home. The garden was illumined by dozens of tall torches, their flames flickering in the evening air. The garden itself turned out to be rather ordinary, a very small plot with a few rose bushes and a couple of statuary. The garden of her family's home back in Sydney had been much larger and more ornate.

Yet with the moon casting its silvery glow around them, the scent of the ocean wafting on the soft breeze, along with the fact that she and Ethan were alone, she didn't care if she were standing on a patch of dusty dirt. She stared out into the darkness, then closed her eyes as a sense of peace stole over her, something she hadn't felt in a long time. Not since she'd shared that special evening with Ethan so many months ago.

After a few moments she opened her eyes to see Ethan staring at her. "I'm sorry," she said, facing him. "You must think I'm an odd duck, coming out here with you and then not saying a word."

"No. To be honest, I was enjoying the quiet."

"So was I. It's very peaceful here."

"Yes it is. Peaceful . . . and beautiful." He raised his hand and briefly touched her cheek with his fingertip, only to withdraw it quickly.

"I'm sorry," he took a step back, looking contrite. "I shouldn't have done that."

"No," she said, once she caught her breath, which had suddenly escaped her. "It's all right."

"I just couldn't help myself." He held up his hands, palms facing her. "But I don't want you to think I go around touching women all the time." A smile twitched on his lips. "Or *kissing* them. I assure you my mother raised me better than that."

Spontaneously she reached out and touched his arm. "It's okay. I didn't mind."

"You didn't?"

"No. Actually, it was very . . . nice. The touch *and* the kiss." She smiled, and it warmed her heart when he smiled in return.

"There you are."

Startled, Jillian spun around to see a short, slightly round woman standing behind them.

"I'm so glad I found you, Ethan," she continued. "I asked Mary Burns where you had gone off to, but strangely enough she wouldn't give me a straight answer. Finally Charles told me where you were." She glanced at Jillian, then back to Ethan. "I'm sorry. Am I interrupting something?"

"Not at all," Ethan said, casting Jillian a knowing look. Then he placed his hand on the other woman's shoulder. "Jillian, this is my mother, Bessie Vincent.

"Mother, this is Jillian um, Jillian—"

"Jillian Sanders," Jillian provided.

"Sanders . . . Sanders. That name sounds so familiar." Bessie put a gloved finger to her lips. "Oh, I know. Are you related to the family that owns Sanders Shipping?"

Surprised, Jillian nodded. "Yes. My father owns . . . *owned* the company." Then her gaze went to Ethan, and her spirits plummeted into a dark abyss. She suddenly realized why the name Vincent also sounded familiar. Vincent *and* Son. The most prosperous shipping company in San Francisco.

She had fallen head over heels for the son of her biggest competitor.

Chapter Five

"Owned?" Bessie asked Jillian. "He is no longer with the company?"

"No, our family is still in the shipping business." Jillian paused, and Ethan watched as the spark that had been so bright in her eyes moments before grow dim. "He passed away a few months ago."

"Oh dear." Sadness crept into his mother's eyes. "I'm so sorry for your loss." After a few seconds of silence, Bessie looked up at him expectantly.

Shaking off his surprise at finding out the woman of his dreams was the daughter of his father's biggest rival, he came back to attention. "May I also offer my condolences?"

"Thank you," Jillian replied.

"I've heard my husband mention your family's company several times," Bessie said. "Actually, I believe the name has come up rather frequently in the past few weeks."

Ethan was quick to intervene. "Mother, I doubt Miss Sanders is interested in Father's work habits." And his father would be livid if he knew his wife was discussing any aspect of the business with anyone, especially the daughter of the man whose company he vowed to put out of business.

"Actually, I'm very interested," Jillian responded.

"You are?" both Ethan and his mother replied in unison. Ethan was particularly surprised, since most of the women he met—whether they were the wives or the daughters or even second cousins twice removed of a successful businessman—were interminably bored with the talk of family business, regardless of what that business might be. They were far more curious about fashion and sewing and social events than the intricacies of balancing books and creating ship manifests.

But here was Jillian, looking more than politely interested by the mere mention of her father's company. Indeed she looked extremely curious.

Then she seemed to backtrack. "I mean, well . . . see my brother has taken over the company since my father's death. And I've become his assistant. In an unofficial capacity, of course."

"Ah," Bessie said. "How dreadfully boring that must be for you."

"Yes. But tragedy does have a way of pulling families together. I'm just doing my bit to help out."

"And I'm sure you're doing magnificently well," Bessie replied.

Ethan remained silent during the ladies' exchange. There was something not quite right in Jillian's responses. Her expression, which had been as open as a well-read book when they were alone, was now completely shuttered. Even a bit defensive, as if she felt under attack somehow. His mother, though normally a sensitive woman, seemed unaware of Jillian's discomfort.

"Ethan dear, we should be on our way," Bessie said, turning to her son. "I wanted to turn in early tonight."

He looked at Jillian. There was so much they needed to say to each other, even more now that this revelation had come to light. But this wasn't the time or the place. "Go on ahead, Mother. I'll be with you shortly."

After her departure, he turned to Jillian. She looked him in the eye, her steely expression setting him back. "I'd like to go inside, please. I believe I've had enough fresh air for the night."

Silently he escorted her back inside, then turned to her. "We need to talk."

"I don't think we have anything to say. Consorting with the competition isn't exactly smart business sense, is it?"

"Jillian—"

"Your mother's waiting."

He held her gaze a moment longer, then relented. "We will talk about this, Jillian. I can promise you that." With that he walked away, vowing to meet with her tomorrow. She had just come back into his life after months of wishing he could see her again. He wasn't about to let her go now.

After Mary and Charles had dropped Jillian off at the hotel, she rushed through the lobby up to her room, slammed the door behind her and leaned against it. For the first time since she realized who Ethan was, she let herself breathe. Placing her hand on her stomach, she inhaled deeply.

She walked over to the tiny desk situated in the corner of the room and sat down behind it. Right there on top of a short stack of papers was a single page with the words *Vincent & Son Shipping* written on top of it. Beneath those words she had listed detailed information about the company. The only company that could be a real threat to the American branch of Sanders Shipping.

She dropped her head into her hands. Of all the men in this city, why did she have to fall for Ethan Vincent?

Suddenly she looked up. What if he'd known all along? What if he had only feigned interest in her so he could ferret out information about her company? What if his asking her to accompany him to the garden had been nothing more than a spying session disguised as a romantic interlude? What if he had marked her as a target from the very beginning?

Immediately she dismissed the thought. Ethan couldn't be duplicitous. He was too kind, too charming . . . too *open*. At least . . . she didn't want to believe it.

There was something about him, however, other than his charm and good looks that drew her to him. Something about him was . . . safe. Secure. She hadn't felt secure in such a long, long time.

Picking up the piece of paper, she stared at it for a moment. This wasn't about her, it was about the company, she had to remember that. About her family, and mostly about her father's legacy. She couldn't put everything in jeopardy over silly romantic notions. Thanks to Roland's complete disinterest in the family business, whether Sanders Shipping succeeded—or failed—was up to her. Although she wanted to trust Ethan, she knew she couldn't.

She wouldn't take that risk.

In the wee hours of the morning, while darkness still shrouded the city, Roland Sanders stumbled into the lobby of the Legion Hotel. With unsteady steps he ascended the staircase and swayed to his room. Fumbling with the doorknob, he finally opened the door and fell inside.

He lay on the floor a few moments while the world spun around him. By jove he was off his face tonight. His pockets were also empty, having spent the last six hours drinking and gambling. It seemed the Americans enjoyed their lager and cards just as much as the blokes back in Sydney.

When the room came to a standstill, he pushed himself off the floor. As quietly as possible he made his way to the bed. It wouldn't do to wake up

Jilly next door. She definitely would *not* approve of his evening's activities. Falling back on the bed, he frowned. How he was sick of being under her thumb, always having to be accountable to her. She was more tyrannical than their father had been.

His mind drifted back in time, back to when he and Jilly were children. Even then his father had been all about business. Jilly had taken to it right away, loving every moment she spent in their father's company, talking about shipments and figures and voyages overseas, and how Sanders Shipping would someday rule the world.

Roland had never shared that closeness. Figures confused him, and the ships made him horribly seasick. Jealousy twisted inside him as he remembered Jilly sitting on their father's lap, telling her how precious she was, how she was his favorite child, how she would accomplish great things one day.

He'd never said that to Roland.

From the time he could remember he had been a disappointment to his father. When he wasn't being outright ignored by him, Roland was at the receiving end of his harsh tongue, and at times, his heavy hand. James Sanders had all but written his son off by the time he was thirteen.

If Roland had his way he would sell the business, take the profits, and head straight back to

Sydney. Sanders Shipping had been nothing but a huge albatross hanging over his life. A legacy he had to live up to, but knew he couldn't. His father had reminded him of that fact nearly every day.

Which was why he had been shocked the day James Sanders' final request was read, naming Roland as the head of the American branch of the company. It had to be a misprint, a mistake, an error. Never would his father have entrusted his son with such an important position.

Of course, not that Roland ever had the chance to be in that position.

From the time they set foot on American soil, Jilly had been in charge. Just as she always was. The will made no difference—she felt the same way his father did. That he was a failure. A ne'er do well.

A waste of space.

Well, he'd prove them right. He always had. Why should geographical location change anything? Jilly would run the company, and he would be a figurehead, all the time plowing his way through every bar, every game, every woman in San Francisco.

That was the only legacy he knew how to successfully fulfill.

Chapter Six

"Jilly, don't you think you should be living somewhere less . . . unseemly?"

"There's nothing wrong with this hotel," Jillian responded as she turned her attention back to her desk.

"Not if you're a transient," Mary mumbled. She removed her hat and laid it on the small, neatly made bed. "You've been in San Francisco for two months now. Why haven't you and Roland sought other accommodations? It's not like you can't afford it." She cast Jillian a skeptical look. "You can afford to move, can't you?"

"Of course I—we can," Jillian snapped. At Mary's surprised expression Jillian forcibly softened her tone. "Finances aren't the reason Roland and I haven't moved yet."

"Then what is the reason?"

Jillian paused. Should she mention how running Sanders Shipping while keeping up the pretense of Roland being an active and responsible part of the company was cutting in to her free time? Should she explain how her brother seemed perfectly satisfied to live the rest of his life at the Legion Hotel, drinking and carousing at his leisure? Or maybe she should confess how desperately she was trying to avoid Ethan Vincent, refusing to see him each of the three times he had called on her at the hotel?

In fact, staying cooped up in her room seemed to solve all her dilemmas quite nicely.

"Jilly? Are you even listening to me?"

"Yes, Mary, I'm listening. I'm just not ready to move. Neither is Roland."

"Well," her friend replied, picking at one of the many loose threads on the thin, cream colored bedcover. "I can see why you have fallen in love with this particular room. Why, a girl would hardly notice the scuffed wainscoting or the crack in the window."

"That's not a crack. It's hardly more than a chip."

Mary jumped up from the bed and went over to Jillian. "What are you hiding from?"

"I'm not hiding from anything," Jillian said, keeping her attention focused on the ledgers in front of her.

"Don't lie to me, Jilly. I'm your oldest friend." Mary placed her hand gently on Jillian's shoulder. "And your dearest, I hope."

Jillian turned to see the concerned expression etched on her friend's features. "You are, Mary. My best friend."

"Then why can't you be honest with me? Why can't you tell me why you're avoiding everyone and everything?"

Jillian averted her eyes. Mary's question was fair. Jillian had never kept secrets from her best friend before. But this time was different. Mary wouldn't understand the pressure Jillian was under. Or worse, her friend would try to help her, and if she did then she'd become involved in her and Roland's problems. It would make a complicated situation even more convoluted. Better to keep family business in the family, even when one of the family members was the source of the problem.

"You've also brushed off Ethan Vincent," Mary continued, tearing into Jillian's thoughts.

Jillian's gaze shot to Mary. "Ethan and I barely know each other. How can I brush off someone whose acquaintance I'm most unfamiliar with?"

"No, the question is, how can you brush off someone you're obviously smitten with?"

"I am *not* smitten." Jillian touched the smooth round end of the pen that protruded from the inkwell at the corner of her desk. Even as she protested to Mary, Ethan's handsome image drifted through her mind.

"I saw you. I saw the way you looked at him, the way he looked at you. You two are perfect together."

"And you're romantically deluded. Not everyone can have a fairy tale life like you, Mary."

"I do not have a fairy tale life. Far from it." Mary let out a sigh. "But I am *happy*. I want you to be happy too."

Jillian blindly thumbed through a sheaf of papers. "I'm . . . content."

"Now who's deluding who?" After a few moments hesitation, Mary walked over to the bed and picked up her hat. She put it carefully on top of her head and stuck a pearl encrusted hat pin through the material. "I know you loved your father very much. But you have to move on. He wouldn't want you wasting your life away in a drafty hotel. And when you're ready to live again, I'll be here."

Touched by her friend's care and devotion, Jillian rose from her chair and crossed the room. She embraced Mary in a tight hug. "Thank you for caring."

"I'll always care. Charles and I will always be here for you."

Jillian stepped back. "Charles barely knows me."

"Then why don't we rectify that? Come over to our house for the evening meal tonight. You and my husband can become better acquainted." She held up her hand when Jillian began to protest. "I won't take no for an answer. Be at my house at six o'clock sharp. You know how I detest tardiness." With a flip of her linen shawl, she flashed a grin and breezed out the door before Jillian could say another word.

Jillian sank onto her bed. She didn't have time for an evening out. She had invoices to complete. A courier to contact. A captain to consult. A brother to argue with, if he ever showed up again.

He was like a little child sometimes. She loved him, but his irresponsibility was becoming intolerable.

She brought her fingertips to the bridge of her nose. She was so tired, tired of everything. Of trying to run a business in secret. Of fighting with Roland every time she saw him. Of trying to put the image and memories of Ethan Vincent out of her mind on an almost hourly basis.

Maybe Mary was right. She needed a break.

Standing up she went to her wardrobe and opened it, then selected a sage green evening dress.

Mary was her friend, and by extension, so was Charles. She could be herself with them. She could drop all pretenses and have a pleasant evening, something she hadn't experienced in ages.

Ethan sat on a wooden crate, a pencil in his mouth and a pad of paper in his hand. He sized up the grand ship in front of him, taking in the majesty of her mainsail as the force of the wind made it billow. He applied the tip of the pencil to his drawing and shaded the left side of the sail, making it more three dimensional.

He continued to work, adding small details to the picture—the rays of the sun fading in the west, the glow of a little boy's cheek as he and his grandfather watched the tide come in near the docks, the unruliness of a sailor's long beard as he walked up the gangplank to board the ship, one of the finest in the Vincent and Son fleet.

Finishing the picture, he held it out in front of him and eyed it critically. Not his best work, not even close. No surprise there—he'd come out here to the family docks to clear his mind. Drawing had always done that for him, especially while inhaling the crisp salty air of the ocean. But how could he concentrate on the subject in front of him when all his mind's eye could see was Jillian Sanders?

His fingers gripped the pencil. Jillian's refusal to see him the three times he had gone to her hotel last week had hit a nerve. How many rebuffs was one man was supposed to take with good grace? Yes, their families' companies were in business against each other, but did that mean he and Jillian couldn't even speak to each another? She was being ridiculous.

"Excuse me. Mr. Vincent?"

Ethan looked up to see Mary Burns standing over him. He quickly stood up, awkwardly clutching his sketchbook to his waist. "Mrs. Burns," he said, catching a better hold on his drawings.

"Your mother said I might find you here."

Strange. Why would Mary Burns pay a visit to his mother? "I'm surprised you would come down here," he said, taking in her delicate frame for a moment. "The docks aren't exactly a place one expects to find a lady taking a late afternoon stroll."

"True." She glanced around. "But I assure you I feel quite at home here. My father was a sailor."

"I didn't know that."

"Oh yes, back in Sydney. He worked for Sanders Shipping. That's how I met Jilly, actually." She smiled. "Ah. I can tell by the expression on your face that I've intrigued you."

"And I can see you don't miss very much."

"You're right. I don't."

"What exactly can I do for you, Mrs. Burns?"

"No, no, Mr. Vincent, it's not what you can do for me. It's what I can do for you."

Chapter Seven

The evening hadn't even started yet, but Jillian didn't think things could get any worse.

The first mishap occurred when she'd started to dress and realized her silk stockings were torn. Checking inside the small chest of drawers in her hotel room she discovered all three pairs of her stockings were ruined. There was no time for her to purchase a new pair at the local mercantile.

Yanking on the pair that were in the best shape, she finished dressing, then began to arrange her hair. While she was pinning up the first curl she heard a noise next door.

Roland had returned.

Dropping her brush, she jumped up from her

seat, left the room and went to his door, knocking her knuckles hard against it.

No answer.

She rapped again, this time more insistently. Finally the door opened. Roland appeared, leaning against the door frame. Actually he appeared to be hugging the wood, as if he needed assistance to remain upright. His clothes were in complete disarray and his red hair was standing out in unkempt tufts on his head.

"Roland! You look terrible."

He lifted his head and squinted at her through half-closed eyes. "And you look ridiculous."

Jillian scowled. "What a childish response."

"Not childish. Truthful. Let me guess, you're a trendsetter now. Soon all the ladies of San Francisco will be wearing their hair only halfway piled up on their heads."

Jillian's hand went to her hair. "I was preparing for an evening out," she said defensively, realizing Roland's assessment was accurate. She must have looked beyond ridiculous standing in the hotel hallway, her hair a mess and her feet clad in stockings dotted with holes.

"An evening out? You?" Roland chuckled, only to hiccup in the middle of it. "I find that hard to believe."

"Will you please let me in?" Jillian said, glancing around the thankfully deserted hallway. But she couldn't count on it remaining empty for long. "I'd rather continue this conversation in private."

"I'd rather not continue it at all."

Jillian let out an exasperated breath. "Roland, for goodness sake! Why must you be so difficult?"

He gave her a half smile, then blew out a breath of air so foul with alcohol and smoke she thought she might faint right on the spot. "I'm not the one being difficult," he said.

"Just forget it! I'm through trying to talk sense into you. You can waste away for all I care!" Spinning on her heel she stomped off to her room, slamming the door behind her.

Anger filtered through every pore, causing her body to shake. Why was he behaving this way? Did he care so little about her and their family that he couldn't lift a finger to help her with the business? Did he care so little about himself, even?

Hot tears of frustration coursed down her cheeks as she sat in front of the mirror. She should just send a note to Mary declining her invitation, saying she was ill or too tired or something. But Jillian knew that wouldn't work. Mary would be over within the hour wanting to know what was wrong. She didn't think she could take another Mary Burns inquisition.

Sniffing, she wiped her tears, swallowed her

emotions, and concentrated on repairing her hair. Better to put everything out of her mind and feign happiness tonight. She would eat supper, visit with Mary and Charles, then come back to her room. She would contemplate the disaster otherwise known as her family when she returned.

Securing the last hairpin in place, she surveyed her reflection in the mirror. Her eyes were swollen, her cheeks were red, and her hair was lopsided.

It was the best she could do.

Gathering her purse and her shawl, she turned down the oil lamp, cloaking the room in the dim light of dusk that streamed through the window. Taking a deep breath, she left the room, determined to be gay and carefree—even if it killed her.

Ethan swirled his drink in the crystal snifter, watching the amber liquid slosh against the fine glass. He glanced at Charles, who was seated directly across from him. They were sitting in front of the fireplace in the Burns' parlor, the crackle of the flames reverberating through the silence of the room. Ethan cracked a half smile at Charles, who returned it, but didn't say anything in response.

The man was very, very quiet. A perfect foil to

his wife, Ethan mused as he brought his drink to his lips. Mary was as chatty as Charles was mute.

"Supper is nearly ready," Mary said as she breezed into the room. "Lin assures us we're in for a culinary treat, straight from her home country of China." She sat down in the burgundy upholstered chair next to her husband. "I've never had Chinese food before. Have you, Mr. Vincent?"

"No, I haven't had the pleasure."

"We were so lucky to hire Lin, weren't we Charles?"

Charles nodded.

"She's a wonderful cook, and runs an impeccable household. I don't know what we'd do without her."

Ethan pulled out his pocket watch. 6:20.

"I wonder what's taking Jilly so long?" Mary said, echoing Ethan's thoughts. "I hope nothing has happened to her."

He hoped nothing had happened to her either. Perhaps she had found out he was here, and decided not to come. The thought left a taste in his mouth far more bitter than the brandy he was imbibing.

"Would you like another drink, Mr. Vincent?" Mary asked.

"No, thank you. And please, call me Ethan."

"Ethan it is." She paused, giving him a smile. "I caught a glimpse of your sketch."

"My sketch?"

"The one of the ship you were sketching at the docks."

"Oh that," he said. "I was just fooling around."

"I thought it was very good. You have a gift for drawing. One I'm sure many people are envious of."

"Hardly," he mumbled, swirling his drink again. "There's not much use for artistry in the business world."

"Oh, I don't know about that. What do you think, Charles?"

Charles opened his mouth to speak, but was interrupted by a knock at the door. Ethan watched as a slim, gray haired butler appeared out of nowhere and headed for the front of the house. After a few moments he came back in the room, a stunned expression on his face. He then moved to the side.

Ethan's jaw dropped at what he saw.

The woman was covered in mud. She was missing one shoe, the stocking on her foot was ripped and exposing her bare toes. Her hat had been shoved to the side of her head and thick, frizzy locks of her hair draped over her shoulders. A dark streak of dirt was smeared on her left cheek. A resigned, weary look haunted her blue eyes.

"Mr. and Mrs. Burns," the butler said, after clearing his throat. Twice. "Miss Jillian Sanders has arrived."

Chapter Eight

Jillian wanted to die right then and there. Or at the very least, turn tail and run. Even in her most horrible nightmares she'd never been so embarrassed. It was bad enough Mary and Charles had to see her in such a wretched state. But sitting right across from them, his mouth agape in what she assumed was shock and in what she hoped wasn't revulsion, was Ethan Vincent. He and Charles both shot up from their chairs.

Why didn't God just end her misery now?

"Good heavens Jilly!" Mary exclaimed, dashing over to her. "What on earth happened to you?"

"Are you okay?" Ethan added, moving toward her.

"It's . . ." She paused to blow out a strand of damp hair that had snuck its way into her mouth. "A long story."

"Well come in here and sit by the fire," Mary said, escorting Jillian to the parlor. She gave her friend's appearance another quick appraisal and frowned. "No, wait, on second thought lets get you upstairs. Charles, be a dear and fetch Lin. Tell her to meet us upstairs with a basin of hot water. And lots of washing cloths."

Jillian let Mary lead her up the stairs. She ascended them unevenly because of her missing shoe. She didn't cast a backward look at Ethan. Out of all the people in San Francisco, why did he have to witness her disgrace?

"Jilly, darling, tell me what happened," Mary asked when they reached her room. She began to untangle the hat from the mess of knots in Jillian's hair. "We were worried something had happened to you."

"Something did," Jillian muttered.

"Well, of course it did, I can see that. There, its out." She tossed the ruined hat to the floor. "You look like you've been for a roll in a mud pit."

"Basically, yes."

Both women turned as the door opened. A

short woman with dark hair and slanted eyes entered the room, carrying a basin. Without a word she set the basin down, turned to her mistress and Jillian, then bowed at the waist.

"That will be all Lin," Mary said.

Lin cast Jillian a quizzical look before leaving them alone in the room.

Mary took a white cloth and soaked it in the water, wrung it out, and handed it to Jillian. "So you were rolling in a mud pit . . ." her voice trailed off in expectation for Jillian to pick up the story.

"Actually the carriage did." She accepted the cloth and brought it to her face, wiping away the grime. "The axel broke as soon as the driver pulled away from the hotel. It spooked the horse, which ran hither and yon through town. Then the driver got it under control, only to pull too hard on the reins, which caused the horse to turn sharply and dump over the carriage." She looked at the mud covered cloth and winced. "Unfortunately the only way to get out was to climb out of the side, which had become the roof, so to speak."

"Oh how dreadful."

"Not as dreadful as when I landed on the ground, lost my footing and fell into a mud puddle. Oh, and I took the driver with me. Poor man was just trying to help."

A funny look crossed Mary's face.

"Don't you laugh. Don't you *dare* laugh."

"I'm not laughing," Mary replied, then bit her bottom lip until it turned white.

That only fueled Jillian's irritation. "This is all your fault."

Mary looked appropriately shocked. "My fault?"

"If you hadn't invited me over for supper none of this would have happened. I wouldn't have been rushing to get over here, I wouldn't have taken the first shoddy looking carriage I could find, and I wouldn't be standing in your sitting room, my dress ruined, not to mention my pride."

"Your pride? Jilly, we're all friends. You don't have to be embarrassed about this."

"Did you forget about Mr. Vincent downstairs?"

Mary froze in the middle of squeezing out another rag. "Actually, his presence did slip my mind."

Jillian turned to her. "What is he doing here anyway? You said tonight would be a chance for me to get to know Charles better. You didn't say anything about another guest."

"He was an afterthought," Mary said, still wringing the cloth even though it was devoid of water.

"I'm sure he would appreciate that sentiment."

"Oh, Jilly, you know what I mean. I ran into him down at the docks—"

"What were you doing at the docks?"

"Just taking a stroll."

"At the *docks?* You haven't strolled on the docks since you were a young girl."

Mary thrust the cloth at her. "What does it matter why I was there? The point is I ran into Ethan and invited him for supper. He accepted."

Jillian eyed her friend skeptically. "So it's Ethan now, is it?"

"He's a very nice man. But I think you know that already. Here, let's get you out of those clothes. I have a lovely azure gown that will fit you perfectly."

Jillian turned around and let Mary unfasten her dress. "I know all I need to know," she said, clutching the front of the gown to her as she turned around to face Mary. "He's a Vincent."

Mary blinked. "Why should that matter?"

"He's a business competitor." Jillian turned back around. "I knew you wouldn't understand," she mumbled.

"No, I don't. His family being in the shipping business is just one more thing you two have in common." Mary picked up a silver-backed brush from her vanity and handed it to Jillian.

Jillian accepted it. “And that’s exactly why we shouldn’t take our relationship any further.”

Mary hesitated, then shook her head. “You’re right. I don’t think I’ll ever understand you, Jilly. I’ll send Lin to you with the dress.” She looked at Jillian’s feet. “And fresh stockings. And a pair of shoes.” She met Jillian’s gaze. “Supper is still warm, if you’re hungry.”

“Will Ethan still be here?”

With a chastising look Mary replied, “Should I send him home? Pack up his supper and direct him on his way?”

Letting out a dejected sigh, Jillian’s shoulders slumped. “No. That would be rude in the extreme. I’ll be down as soon as I can.”

Mary’s countenance brightened. “Splendid. I’ll tell the men.” With that she flounced out of the room.

“*Splendid*,” Jillian mocked, making a face as she said the word. She stepped out of the dress, then sat down on the chartreuse chaise and peeled off the remnants of her stocking. It would be a long time before she accepted another invitation from Mary, she vowed.

A very, very long time.

Chapter Nine

Ethan stared at the plate in front of him, unsure of the pile of food lying there. He'd never had Chinese cooking before, and after inspecting the dish being served, he wasn't sure he could bring himself to try it.

Charles seemed to have the same reaction. Ethan watched as the slender man poked the lump with his fork cautiously, almost as if he expected the food to retaliate.

"It's called Lo Mein," Mary said, taking her own fork and twirling a few strands of noodles on it.

"Is that Chinese for worms?" Charles remarked

dryly, uttering more words at that moment than he had the entire night.

Ethan suppressed a chuckle. It certainly looked like there was a load of worms on his plate. He half expected the tan strands to start wiggling at any moment.

"Sorry I'm late."

Ethan looked up from perusing his meal. Then he immediately stood.

Jillian looked beautiful. The pale blue dress she had changed into only enhanced her bright blue eyes. It didn't matter that the gown seemed a little too snug in the waist and slightly too big at the square neckline. Nor did he care that her hair, neatly arranged in a serviceable topknot, wasn't exactly the height of fashion.

To him she was the loveliest woman he knew.

Gracefully she walked over to the table. The butler, Stearns, pulled out a chair for her. Ethan also sat back down. Although she sat opposite from him, she never met his eyes, instead keeping her gaze directly on her plate.

Suddenly, she frowned. "What is this?" she queried, lowering her head to get a closer look at the meal.

"Lo Mein," Ethan, Mary and Charles said in unison.

"It's quite good, actually." Mary scooped another small pile of noodles into her mouth, then reached for her napkin. "But a bit messy."

"Naturally," Jillian said in a low, resigned tone.

The room grew silent, with only the occasional slurping sound heard. The food was surprisingly delicious, along with the green tea served in small, unusual cups without handles. Mary explained that Lin had brought the set with her from China.

Despite the appetizing and interesting meal, prickles of discomfort began to bother Ethan. Not only had Jillian not acknowledged him, she hadn't even looked at him. Had he grown another eyeball that he wasn't aware of?

Then Mary, apparently feeling the need to start a conversation, asked Jillian, "Did you know Ethan's an artist?"

Jillian's hand paused as she reached for her teacup. Quickly she cast a glance in his direction, then immediately focused on the cup as if it would disappear if she didn't look at it. "No. I was unaware of Mr. Vincent's artistic talents."

"Ethan," he said, looking directly at her, willing her to look at him. To see him the same way she had before they discovered who their families were. She was erecting a wall of formality in an effort to keep him out. And he hated it.

"Ethan is madly talented, I can assure you," Mary continued. "I've seen his work. Well, a sketch really, but it was a marvelous one. I believe it was of the *Silverhook* wasn't it?" she looked at Ethan expectantly.

One of Jillian's delicately shaped eyebrows raised, showing her first inkling of interest in him the entire evening. "One of your ships?"

"Yes." He picked up his tea. "I can show you the drawing of it someday, if you'd like."

Surprise flashed across her features. "You'd show the competition pictures of your ships?"

"Jillian, you're hardly competition—"

"Excuse me?" Jillian dropped her napkin on her plate.

"Charles dear," Mary interjected, her voice a bit too loud as she stood up. "Help me take the dishes to the kitchen."

Charles furrowed his brows. "But Mary, we never help in the kitchen—"

"Now, Charles."

Without another word Charles also rose from his seat, and he and Mary disappeared from the room.

Now Jillian was looking at Ethan directly. Pointedly staring at him, actually.

"Apparently what I said came out wrong,"

Ethan started. "I know Sanders Shipping is our competitor—"

"But not a serious one, in your estimation."

"Yes, a serious one, but—"

"I think it's time I left." Jillian stood up from the table. "Give Mary and Charles my regrets."

"Jillian—stop."

She froze at the edge in his voice.

"Now that I have your attention . . . it's time to have our talk."

Jillian twisted her fingers together and squeezed them until they turned white. She didn't want to talk to him. She didn't even want to be near him. At least that's what she kept telling herself. But her mind and her heart were saying different things. Many different things.

His expression softened as he rose from his chair. Swiftly he walked around the table until he was standing beside her. She looked up into his face, remembering the softness of his kiss. A kiss she'd replayed in her mind a million times over. If only she hadn't let him get close to her. Hadn't let him kiss her. Hadn't let him sneak into the fringes of her heart, threatening to bury himself in there forever.

Dear Lord, what was she going to do?

He touched her upper arm, letting his fingers slide to her elbow in a move that made her shiver. "Don't leave," he said, his voice as smooth as the sea on a perfectly calm day. "I understand the Burns have a lovely balcony."

Not the balcony again. "Ethan, no . . ."

"You're mouth is telling me no," he said, hooking her hand through his bent elbow. "But you're eyes are telling me yes."

Involuntarily she closed her eyes. At the same time she felt him leading her forward. Her resistance was eroding quickly. Riding on a wave of helplessness, she opened her eyes, and followed him.

Chapter Ten

All Jillian noticed as she and Ethan stepped out on the balcony was his muscular arm underneath her hand. The tangy scent of his aftershave as the ocean breeze wafted around them. The tension ebbing away from her neck and shoulders.

"It's a beautiful evening," he said, leading her to the edge of the porch. "The sky looks like a blanket of black velvet."

"With diamonds sprinkled all over it."

"Spoken like a woman with a true artistic eye."

"I don't know about that. I can barely draw a circle, much less anything else. I've always been more practically minded."

"Well, that's something I wish I was. Or at

least, my father does." He released her arm. But instead of putting his hands on the wrought iron rail in front of him, he slipped his arm around her waist.

Her breath caught. But she didn't move away from him.

They stared onto the street below. There were a few people milling around and walking down the boardwalk, their conversations a muted hum in her ears. What was she doing, allowing him this close? He had taken liberties with her that no man had a right to, yet she couldn't bear to push him away. His arm around her was firm and strong. She could feel the warmth of his body against hers as they stood side by side.

Then he turned her toward him, and she was jolted back to reality. "Ethan . . . stop."

"Jillian." It was all there in his utterance of her name. The depth of his emotions for her—she felt them all the way to her core.

Which was why she had to put an end to this. "This isn't going to work."

"What?" he asked, reaching up and touching a stray tendril of her hair. He wound it around his finger, then gently let it go.

"Us. Together." She gulped as he traced her cheek with the back of his hand. "W-we can't pursue this any further."

"Why not? I like you . . . and even though you're doing everything you can to make me think otherwise, I know you like me."

"Ethan, please. I'm serious."

"And that's your problem, Jilly. You're too serious."

"I have to be. I have a lot of responsibilities."

"So do I." He frowned, dropping his hand and taking a few steps away from her. "I'm the 'Son' in Vincent and Son. Maybe I should be more serious."

"No," she blurted, surprising herself. "I mean . . ." She sighed deeply. "I wish I could be more like you, Ethan. I wish I could just let it all go."

"Let what go?" He tilted up her chin and gazed into her eyes. "You're carrying a heavy burden, Jillian Sanders. I can see it. Tell me what's wrong. I want to help you."

The urge to explain everything nearly overwhelmed her. More than anything she wanted to trust him. But how could she explain about Roland? How could she hand over to her biggest competitor the ammunition he needed to sink her company?

She averted her eyes and stepped out of his arms, moving over to the opposite end of the balcony. Suddenly the soft strains of violin music reached her ears. So faint at first that she thought she imagined them. But then they grew louder. She looked down on the street below where a lone violinist was stroking his bow across the stringed instrument, an open case next to his feet.

She felt Ethan come up behind her, his arms wrapping around hers and drawing her back against him. "Shh," he whispered against her ear when she tried to move away. "This is how you let it go, Jillian." He nodded to the musician on the street. "Just listen to the serenade."

Jillian took a deep breath, hesitant. Then she realized she deserved this, a brief moment of happiness. She'd deal with the repercussions of this night later. She leaned against him as they listened to the music. Right now she was going to follow Ethan's lead, and simply enjoy.

Chapter Eleven

With the toe of his boot Dell Watkins kicked the lifeless body, making sure the man on the ground was dead. The pistol in Dell's hand was still warm, and the smell of gunpowder overwhelmed the small, dank cave. He wiped his nose on the back of his sleeve and stared at the well-dressed man, his black suit flawless—except for the dark, wet bloodstain increasing on the lapel of his jacket.

It was the man's own fault, Dell reasoned. Sure, John Palmer had been his attorney, and had been instrumental in arranging his escape from that hellhole of a jail Harold Vincent had put him in. Palmer had also been the one to hide the money Watkins had earned smuggling prohibited goods on Vincent and Son's ships. He had been a good partner, actually.

Until he got greedy.

Dell hunkered down and searched the man's coat, finding a pocket watch, a wallet with a few bills, and a packet of chewing tobacco. He pulled out a plug of the tobacco and tucked it in his mouth, withdrew the bills and flung the wallet aside, then tucked the watch into his ripped pocket.

Rising, he took a look at his surroundings. Small cave, safely hidden away from town. There was a pile of ash on the dusty floor, the remnants of a fire burned out long ago. Maybe a gold miner had dwelled in the cave for a while, searching and wishing to strike it rich. Something Dell had already done. And he hadn't had to break his back to accomplish it.

He wouldn't be here for very long. Just long enough to formulate and carry out his plan of revenge on Harold Vincent. Once he'd ruined the man that had sent him away, he would get his money, sneak on board a ship and sail to Australia. Or China. He didn't care. As long as it was far, far away from San Francisco.

He picked up a fisherman's cap, old and weather beaten. He stroked his matted beard, which had lengthened considerably during his time in jail. He had one more thing to do. One last task to complete before he left.

He cast another glance at Palmer, then spit out a lump of the tobacco. If the man hadn't tried to squeeze more money out of Dell he'd be alive right now. If only he'd stuck with the thirty/seventy split they'd agreed upon up front, he would still be walking and breathing. Dell shrugged.

It didn't pay to be greedy. Palmer learned that lesson the hard way.

"So? Tell me what happened? And I want details, Jilly. No hemming and hawing around like you normally do."

"I don't hem and haw," Jillian replied as she admired a lovely pair of lavender stockings. "And you're being frightfully nosy."

"I have a right to be," Mary said. She and Jillian were shopping at Chong's mercantile together. "After all, I did discover you and Ethan cuddling on my balcony."

Jillian suddenly became interested in the weave of the stocking.

"You're blushing, Jilly." Mary picked up three pairs of the fine silk stockings and sighed. "I knew the two of you would be perfect together."

Jillian cast an annoyed glance. "That was a

rotten trick you pulled on me last night. Inviting Ethan without telling me."

"Someone had to do something. You're too stubborn and he's too nice. You would have never gotten together if it weren't for me."

"We are *not* together—"

"It certainly appeared that way to me."

Turning to her friend, Jillian eyed her sternly. "Mary, I would appreciate it if you wouldn't meddle. Ethan and I are not together and we never will be. Last night was . . ." *Nice. Wonderful. Soothing.* And something she wished would last forever.

"Last night was what?" Mary prodded.

"Happenstance. Something I will make certain never happens again."

"But Jilly—"

"Mary, listen to me. I don't trust very many people in this world. You are one person I do trust. Please, do not give me reason to doubt that. I have my own grounds for not wanting to get involved with Ethan. I ask that you respect that."

Mary paused, then nodded, somewhat reluctantly. "Okay. I'll stop meddling." Her expression grew somber. "I did what I did because I care about you. I want you to be happy. You're not very happy right now."

Extending her hand to Mary's, Jillian clasped

it and gave it an affectionate squeeze. "I know, Mary. And I appreciate it. But I'll be fine."

"Are you sure?"

No. She wasn't sure of anything anymore. Actually, that wasn't true either, she was sure of one thing—she was teetering on the edge of falling in love with Ethan Vincent. And she didn't know what to do about it.

She tamped down her thoughts and patted Mary's hand. "Of course I'm sure," she said, forcing a smile that she knew had to look fake. "Now, let's purchase these stockings."

Ethan stared at the sketch in his hand. He'd fully intended on working on a new drawing of the interior of his ship. But the sketch had turned into something else—someone else. Jillian. He ran his fingertips along the charcoal outline of her lips.

Sitting out on the back balcony of his own home reminded him of last night. What had started out as a shaky evening had ended up truly special. A night he would never forget, and one that he longed to repeat.

He stared out at the port below, listening to the sounds of the sea, sailors, and ships. He remembered what she had said last night, how she wanted to let everything go. And she seemed to, for a brief moment. Until they were interrupted by Mary and Charles. Then she had reverted to her cool demeanor, telling him good night as if they were mere acquaintances, even though they both knew they were much more than that.

He studied his sketch again. Even though he wasn't skilled at portraiture, he somehow had captured the guarded expression in her eyes. The shadows beneath them. The tight, drawn lines at the corners of her mouth. "What are you hiding, Jillian Sanders?" he asked aloud. "What deep secrets lie behind those lovely blue eyes?"

"There you are," Bessie Vincent came out onto the porch, waving a whalebone handled fan in front of her face. "Goodness it's warm today."

Snapping his book shut, Ethan immediately rose from his chair. "August is always warm."

"Yes, but does it really have to be?"

His mother had posed the question with such serious weariness he was compelled to squelch a smile. "I'm sorry, Mother, but I believe it does."

"Well, dreadful weather aside, your father is looking for you. He's in the library, and I must say his mood is rather sour."

"When is it not?"

"Yes, I see you've noticed too." Bessie sat down and flicked her fan back and forth. "I don't know what's gotten into your father as of late. It seems like all he does is grumble and complain about business." An uncharacteristic shadow crossed over her face. "He barely resembles the man I married."

Ethan nodded.

"I remember much happier times, Ethan darling," Bessie continued, staring out over the port, "when your father would talk of other things besides profit and loss margins. When he would come home with a smile on his face instead of a scowl. When we would spend time together, just the two of us." She turned to Ethan, giving him a watery smile that didn't reach her eyes. "You had better run along. Don't keep him waiting."

Ethan leaned forward and kissed her cheek, his heart going out to her pain. But there was nothing he could do. How could he help his parents' relationship when his own relationship with his father was severely strained?

As soon as Ethan opened the door to the library he could see his mother's assessment of her husband's mood was alarmingly accurate.

"They are going to put us out of business!" Harold exclaimed, slamming a sheaf of papers down on his desk.

"Who is?" Ethan asked as he guardedly entered the room, keeping his distance from his fuming father.

"That blasted Sanders Shipping." Harold stormed around his desk. "This is the second time this month they've stolen a contract right out from underneath us." He faced Ethan squarely. "Your mother tells me you're familiar with the Sanders girl."

Ethan eyed him warily. "What are you planning?"

Harold grinned harshly. "A little fishing expedition, son. For the good of the company, of course."

Chapter Twelve

"You want me to spy on Jillian?"

"Not spy, necessarily." Harold retrieved a cigar from his breast pocket. "Just some information gathering. I need to know how they're managing to underbid me. Especially since all their business seems to be done through the company attorney, a fellow named Holland. Then there's the whole mystery behind the head of the company, Roland Sanders. Word is he's been spotted in some very shady establishments since his arrival in town. Perhaps you can also glean some information about that we can use."

Ethan was appalled by his father's request, but

he was in no way surprised by it. "What you're asking me to do is unethical."

"No it's not. It's business, pure and simple."

"There's nothing simple about it. You want me to use Jillian Sanders to find out information you can use against her family's company." He crossed his arms. "I won't do it."

Harold stood, his left eye twitching. "Not even for our family? For the business I spent my entire life building?" Harold took a step toward his son. "Not even for me?"

"No Father. Not even for you."

Harold's eyes narrowed. "You're smitten with this girl, aren't you?"

"She's not a girl, Father, she's a grown woman. And whether I'm smitten with her or not makes no difference. Not in this situation. What you're asking me to do is wrong, and I won't be a part of it."

Harold's eyes turned icy. "Then perhaps you don't want to be a part of this business."

"That's not what I said—"

"But it's what you mean. You've never been that interested in Vincent and Son. You've always had your head in the clouds, or your attention on a sketchbook, making useless drawings."

"They're not useless. They're sketches of ships. Bigger, better, stronger ships."

"Pipe dreams on paper. That's all it boils down to." Harold slowly stepped back, then walked over to his desk. With unnerving calm he sat down, and looked directly at Ethan. "I've never said this to you before, Ethan, but I've always suspected it. Today just settles it in my mind. You're not cut out for this business. I see now that you never were."

"But—"

"As of today I'm relieving you from any responsibility in the company. You can continue to live here with your mother and I, we will support you for the time being. But you'll have to start looking for employment for yourself, because you no longer have a place with Vincent and Son."

A hard lump formed in Ethan's throat. "You can't mean that."

"I mean exactly what I said. I know where your loyalties lie, and they aren't with me." Harold picked up a piece of paper and began to study it.

For a few long, drawn-out moments Ethan stood there in the center of the library, silently begging for his father to speak to him, to acknowledge him, to yell at him even. Anything was better than the chilly silent treatment he was receiving.

"Look at yourself," Ethan finally spoke, struggling to keep the tremble out of his voice. "You've cut me out just because I won't do what you want. What's happening to you, Father? What has made you such a cold, hard man?"

Harold continued to look down at the desk, as if Ethan weren't standing there right in front of him. As if his own son was invisible.

Slowly, Ethan turned and walked out of the room. It was as if he were suffocating, like a pile of cinder bricks was piled upon his chest. He found it hard to breathe, and even the spacious great room of the Vincent home seemed to close in on him. As if in a trance, he started for the door.

"Ethan, darling, where are you going?" his mother called after him as he passed by her.

He didn't answer her. How could he explain what had just happened? How could he tell his mother that he had practically been cut off from his own family?

He headed out blindly into the street and turned to hurry down the boardwalk. He needed to think, needed to sort out this mess. Maybe after a few hours he could return home, talk to his father rationally, and straighten everything out. Certainly Harold Vincent wouldn't hold a grudge against his son forever.

Would he?

* * *

Darkness engulfed the port of San Francisco. The ocean waves lapped against the ships and wooden docks, their rhythm unbroken and in perfect synchronicity.

Roland Sanders dragged himself along the pier. His head pounded, his throat ached, and his body throbbed all over. How had he let it come to this? He brought his hand up to his swollen eye, then gingerly touched the bleeding cut extending over it. This was only a first warning, the thug had said as he paused between punches. Next time would be a whole lot worse.

What could be worse than this? Roland let out a bitter sound, but moaned in the middle of it. More than likely he had broken ribs too. But his physical injuries were paltry compared to the larger problem that hung over him.

Where was he going to come up with one thousand dollars?

His gambling debts had piled high over the past several weeks. Desperate, he had borrowed money from a shady character who dealt with that sort of thing. Roland had almost laughed out loud when he first met the man that referred to himself only as Boxer. He was short, balding, and thin as a whip of black licorice. He also wore glasses that were always slipping down his bulbous nose. The man looked as harmless as a fly.

And harmless he was, until Roland had missed a payment.

Roland had been on a roll, winning left and right, until tonight, when he lost it all, including the loan payment that was already two days overdue. It was at that moment he found out that Boxer didn't appreciate tardiness. He had sent a massive brute after Roland to "teach him a lesson." And it was a lesson all right. A very painful one.

But what was he to do now? He couldn't go begging to Jilly. His pride wouldn't allow it. He had shamed the family name enough in the past. He wasn't about to drag her into his quagmire of problems.

He tilted his head back and let the ocean mist cover him. What did it matter anyway? Jilly was doing just fine with the company, she didn't need him around messing things up for her. It would better for them all if he just left town. He looked down at the inky black water below. *Or maybe I should just leave everyone . . . for good.*

"Now matey, you wouldn't want to be doin' that now, would ya?"

Roland jumped at the creaky voiced man who suddenly appeared next to him. "How do you know what I was planning to do?"

"Well, I'd wager ye were plannin' to jump. Ye had that look in yer eye. The look that tells me yer a man down on his luck."

Roland squinted out of his good eye, trying to get a clear picture of the man. He was hunched over, with a sailor cap perched low on his head, a grizzled beard covering almost all of his face. He smelled like fish and stale tobacco.

"I'm down on my luck all right," Roland muttered, looking away from the man and out into the darkness of the night. "And there's nothing I can do about it."

"Mayhaps not. But mayhaps I can help ye."

Roland snorted. "How could you possibly help me? You're in worse shape than I am."

"Ah, but looks can be deceivin', matey. Don't be dismissin' what ye don't know."

Irritated, Roland turned to him. "Fine, tell me how you can help me."

"Well, my boss has somethin' he needs done. An' I'm thinkin' yer the man fer the job."

"What job?"

"I'll be givin' you the details, but not here. We need to go some place more . . . private, ye see."

Roland shrugged. "All right, I'll go with you. It's not like I have anything left to lose anyway." He followed the bent sailor off the pier and onto the boardwalk. "By the way, what's your name?"

"Palmer," the man replied, not turning around. "John Palmer."

Chapter Thirteen

Ethan rubbed the back of his neck as he walked along the boardwalk. Anxiety gripped his chest like a vise. He was still in a state of shock. His future, which had always been so secure, was now a big question mark. His relationship with his father, which had been volatile at times but never hateful, now seemed permanently damaged.

What was he going to do now?

One thing he certainly wasn't going to do was spy on Jillian's company. Anger replaced anxiety as he thought about Harold's outrageous demand. How could he ask Ethan to be so deceptive? Worse yet, how could he cut him out of the family business—and the family—for doing the right thing? For being honest?

Ethan suddenly realized he didn't know his father anymore. He wondered if he ever had.

He stood there for a moment, breathing in the briny scent of the ocean. He couldn't imagine doing anything else with his life or moving anywhere else. San Francisco, the docks, the ocean—this was his home.

He also couldn't betray Jillian. He had fallen for her, fallen hard. Yes, she was surrounded by a tough veneer, but he could also sense her softer side. The side that appreciated beauty, whether visual, aural, or intellectual. The side that needed nurturing.

He blew out a long, despondent breath. What was he thinking—he was the last person Jillian needed right now. Clutching his overcoat closer to his body, he didn't know if the chill he felt came from the outside air or the emptiness in his soul.

He continued walking, eventually coming upon the Vincent docks. His father's docks. They were empty now. Soft waves lapping against the hull of two ships docked for the night were the only sounds he heard. Never had he felt so alone.

Then out of the corner of his eye he caught a

movement. Two dark figures moving in the shadows.

He wasn't alone after all.

Immediately suspicious, he moved closer to the shadowy forms. They were speaking in very low tones, their heads together as they stood by one of the ships. The hair sprang up on the back of Ethan's neck. There was no reason for anyone to be at the docks at this late hour.

It was difficult to see their faces in the dim light the small sliver of moon provided. But he could see one was tall and thin, while the other wore a dilapidated sailor hat. Ethan relaxed slightly. Perhaps they were new security his father had hired and were giving the ships one last look over before retiring for the night.

But as he approached he realized they weren't checking the ships. It was more like they were examining the vessels, as if they were unfamiliar to them. Ethan slowed his pace, not wanting to alert the men to his presence. But when they turned around sharply and faced him, he realized he was too late.

"Ho there," he said, his guard up. "These are private docks. What business have you here?"

The taller man stepped from the shadows. Ethan drew in a sharp breath. The man's face was puffy and bruised, his bottom lip split and encrusted with dark, dried blood. One eye was nearly swollen shut. He moved on wobbly legs, but from the stench he emanated, Ethan knew his uneven gait was due to imbibing, not his injuries.

The man cleared his throat. “A thousand pardons, sir,” he said, his voice sounding more sober than his movements and scent led Ethan to believe. “I’m afraid I’m lost, and this kind sailor—” He swiveled to gesture to the other man.

But the sailor was gone.

Clearly confused, the drunken man turned back to Ethan. “He was here, I know he was.” Then he seemed to retreat into himself, staring at the ground, mumbling. “Unless I dreamed the entire thing up.”

Ethan shook his head. “No, I saw him too.” He glanced around the docks, but it was as if the sailor had vanished. Ethan looked back at the other man, still wary. “I’m sorry you’re lost, but that’s not my problem. You’re still trespassing. If you need some directions—”

“No. I’ll find my way back on my own.” His words sounded muffled, as if he were having trouble forming them. By the split line in his bottom lip, Ethan could see how speaking could be difficult. “Again. A thousand pardons,” he continued. “I’ll be on my way now.”

Ethan regarded him for a moment as the slim fellow looked around in bewilderment, as if he were still searching for the sailor. There was something familiar about him, something Ethan couldn't quite pinpoint. Something in the voice . . . or was it his face . . .

Then the man spun around and began walking away. Actually he was limping slightly, but Ethan thought he moved faster than humanly possible considering his condition. Soon he too disappeared, just as the sailor had moments before.

With nothing left to do, Ethan started to turn around and head for home when he caught a glimpse of something white on the ground. Bending over, he picked up a handkerchief made of fine linen, but half-caked with what he presumed was dried up blood. Looking back in the direction the other man left in, he gripped the cloth, tucked it in his pocket, and departed the docks.

A short while later, Ethan quietly let himself into the house, not wanting to alert anyone to his presence at this late hour. Especially his father.

He started ascending the staircase when he saw a flicker of light appear to his right. The soft padding sound of his mother's slippers against the stone foyer floor stopped him.

"Ethan, dear. I'm glad you're home." She moved closer to the stairs. "May we talk?"

Nodding, he turned around and followed her into the parlor. She set down her small lamp on a round end table, then lit another one before gesturing for him to sit in the posh high-backed chair across from her own.

"He didn't mean what he said, Ethan," Bessie insisted as he sat down.

"You heard, then?"

"Your father is quite loud, as you well know." She smoothed the folds of her cotton wrapper that covered her short legs. "He's also been very impulsive as of late."

"And angry." Ethan stared at his hands for a moment. "He's changed, Mother."

"I know."

They didn't say anything for a long time, just sat together in the dim room. Finally Bessie spoke. "He loves you, Ethan. Always remember that. No matter what."

"He has a strange way of showing it." Ethan rose from his chair, realizing nothing would be settled tonight. His mother couldn't do anything but give him verbal reassurances. Her soft declarations barely took root against the echo of his father's blistering dismissal.

"Good night, Mother," he said.

Bessie stood up, then tiptoed over and kissed her son on the cheek. "It's time I had a talk with

Harold. This has gone on long enough. Don't you fret about it, dear. You'll always have a place in our home, and in the business. I'll make sure of that."

Ethan regarded her for a moment. Seemingly frail and oblivious on the outside, he knew she possessed a tough interior core. But it would take more than just a talking to by his mother to heal the wounds his father had inflicted on him. Still, he loved her for trying.

In the early hours of the next morning, Ethan felt a sharp tugging on his shoulders. He fought to open his eyes, which were heavy with sleep. "Mother?" He shot to an upright position. "What's wrong?"

"Fire!" his mother cried, her voice shrill. She held a lit oil lamp. It clattered in her quaking hand.

Ethan sprang out of bed, his night shirt billowing behind him. He snatched up his trousers and started yanking them on. "Where?"

"At the docks. Your father has already left." Her lower lip began to tremble. "The ships . . ."

"What about the ships?" He grabbed his boots from the floor. When she didn't answer right away he repeated, "Mother! What about the ships?"

"They're gone." Her tone was flat. "The *Silverhook* and the *Ellen Gale*. They're unsalvageable. I only pray the offices don't go up in flames as well."

A cold knife of fear sliced through Ethan as he shoved his feet into the boots. San Francisco had fallen victim to many savage fires over the years. Property—and lives—had been lost every time.

He saw the frightened expression on his mother's face. Reaching out, he touched her cheek with his palm. "It will be all right, Mother," he told her softly.

"But what if Harold—"

"He won't. Nothing will happen to Father. I'll make sure of it."

Ethan dashed out of the house and headed for the docks. The air was thick with smoke before he even reached his destination. He could see the flames rising from the pier, smell the acrid scent of burning wood and ash. Dozens of men were scattered around, shouting orders, dousing the flames with water from hoses, wooden buckets, tin cups—anything they could get their hands on—desperate to keep the fire confined to the two ships.

His eyes burned and tears squeezed out of them as he searched for his father. Noting a light glowing from the glass-paned window in the warehouse, he ran to the door, threading his way through the valiant group of fire fighters.

"Father!" he called out as he thrust open the door. "Father! Are you in here?"

He received no answer. Undaunted, Ethan rushed into the room and headed for the back where the cargo was stored and inventoried. Looking around the room, his heart sank as he spied his father on the floor, an unlit cigar in his hand.

"Father!" He hurried, then crouched on the floor beside him. "Father, we must leave, now."

Harold stared into the distance as if he was unaware of his son's presence. "It's gone . . . all gone."

"Only ships are gone," Ethan said, grabbing his father's arm. He tried to help him to his feet, but the older man remained firmly rooted to the floor.

"The ships . . . the cargo . . . all of it gone. Up in flames. Poof." He laughed flatly, and the mirthless sound haunted Ethan. "Thousands and thousands of dollars, up in smoke. Ruined. It's all ruined."

"We have other ships. Several ships. And we can build more. But we have to hurry." Ethan gripped his father's arm tighter. "We can't stay here."

His father said nothing.

Ethan glanced out the window. The fire didn't

seem to be spreading toward them, but he didn't want to take any chances. "We're leaving *now*," he said firmly, yanking on Harold's arm. With a mighty pull he dragged his father's corpulent form to a standing position, then took him by the arm and lugged him out of the warehouse.

When they were a safe distance from the burning ships, he slowed his pace, fighting to catch his breath. His father breathed equally as hard. Both men turned and watched as the bright orange blaze consumed the ships. Some of the men had released the vessels from their moorings and were pulling the burning masses of wood and iron by rowboat out to sea, away from the pier.

"I never thought it would end like this," Harold mumbled weakly.

For the first time Ethan noticed the soot covering his father's face. He also saw the red burn mark on the side of his neck, as if a stray ember had blown from the ship and landed on his skin. Ripping a strip of cloth from the bottom of his nightshirt, Ethan wrapped it around Harold's wound.

The two ships had been their best, and had been packed to the rim with cargo. Even if they did rebuild, it would take years to recoup the money they'd lost by losing the vessels. Maybe his father was right. Maybe it was over.

But Ethan refused to believe it. "It's not the end," he said firmly. "We have more ships. We'll rebuild the others." He looked at his father's lifeless eyes. "We will be strong again."

His father stared at the burning wreckage. "Why are you doing this? After what I said to you? After what I did?" He turned to Ethan, and a spark of life entered his eyes again.

"Because we're family," Ethan said. "And your dream is my dream. I think I finally realized that." He wouldn't let this disaster set them back. And if his father didn't have the strength to bring back the company from such dire straights, Ethan would find a way to do so.

He would stake his life on it.

Chapter Fourteen

Jillian stared out her hotel window, horrified by what she saw. She didn't have a clear view of the docks, but she could see the bay, and the huge fireball being towed out to sea.

She didn't have to wonder what happened, she already knew. It was something she'd seen before, back in Sydney. Fortunately not to her father's company.

Two ships lost. And from the direction they were departing from, she suspected they were Vincent and Son ships.

A sick lump formed in her stomach as she continued to look out the open window. The smoke seemed to permeate everything. She wondered if Ethan was down there, among the dark figures milling around on the pier, staring out as the vessels made their final voyage.

Her heart went out to him. Rationally she should be rejoicing. Losing two great ships would be devastating to Vincent financially. Perhaps it would even put the company on the brink of ruin. It opened up a variety of opportunities for Sanders to take advantage of. It wouldn't be too hard to put Vincent and Son out of business for good.

The thought made her head throb.

She closed her window, turned away from the wrenching scene, and climbed into bed. Closing her eyes, she tried to sleep, but all she could see was Ethan's face. She imagined the devastation in his eyes as he watched his father's business turn to ashes. Rolling over on her side, she tried to banish away the negative thoughts. He wasn't her concern, after all.

Except, at that moment, all she longed to do was be by his side, and comfort him.

Bleary eyed, Ethan stared out into the bay, watching the plumes of smoke rise up from the still smoldering frame of the *Ellen Gale*. The other ship had sunk into the sea, but this one seemed to hang on, refusing to succumb to its watery grave.

The morning had dawned gray and foggy. The smell of burned wood and destruction hung thick in the air. The docks were completely abandoned at this early hour. He wiped his forehead with the sleeve of his nightshirt, then looked at the black soot clinging to the linen fabric. He had stayed at the docks all night, sending his father home with an escort a couple hours earlier.

Fatigue seeped into his bones, but he refused to leave. Something was keeping him there. A niggling feeling deep within him, a sense that nothing about this situation was as it appeared to be.

Ethan thought about the night before, about the sailor and the odd gentleman he had found near the ships. Questions hovered in his mind. Was this all an accident? Or was the destruction of the ships due to something else?

He walked toward the edge of the dock where the two vessels had been moored. Kneeling, he scrutinized the ground. What he was searching for he didn't know, but he was compelled to examine every bit of the area.

After a few minutes he noticed something glistening on the edge of the dock. A small, round drop, not much bigger than the pad of his index finger. He touched the substance, rubbing it between his fingertips. It was slick, like oil. Lamp oil, perhaps. He smelled it. Not lamp oil. Some other type of fuel. Looking around, he noticed a few other wet spots with the same consistency as the first one.

What was fuel oil doing near the ships?

He rose slowly, then reached into his pocket for the handkerchief that he had crammed in there the night before. He opened the square fabric, tugging at the stuck parts until they separated. The stains were dark crimson. Blood, just as he thought. He inspected it for traces of the oil, but found none. Yet he did find something else interesting. In the bottom right hand corner of the handkerchief was a monogram. Stitched in a deep green color were two letters: *RS*.

"Ethan."

His head jerked up at the sound of the soft, feminine voice.

Jillian.

Jillian approached Ethan with tentative steps, unsure why she was here. Pain and grief were etched on his face, as if he had lost a loved one instead of two lifeless ships. But his reaction wasn't strange to her, not in the least. She would have felt the same way under the same circumstances.

He turned and faced her, stuffing something in his pocket as he did. The ever present twinkle in his gray eyes was gone. His mouth, often so ready with a smile, was a pale, thin slash.

"What are you doing here?" he asked dully. His expression suddenly turned sharp. "Are you here to gloat? To take pleasure in my family's loss?"

His words cut her deeply, but she couldn't blame him for saying them. "No. That's not why I'm here."

His shoulders slumped. "I shouldn't have said that."

She moved closer to him. "If it makes you feel better to lash out at me, go ahead." She gave him a small smile. "I can take it."

The corner of his mouth lifted. "I'm sure you can." He turned from her and stared out into the bay.

The sun began to rise past the horizon, casting the sky in a soft palette of lavender, pink, and orange hues. The silence stretched between them, but she stayed by his side. Thoughts of Sanders Shipping faded away as they watched the last remnants of the second ship slowly sink into the sea. She heard Ethan sigh wistfully.

"I'm so sorry," she said, her voice barely above a whisper.

"It will take months for us to recoup the losses," he lamented. "Years, even."

"You'll manage it. I know you will."

Without a word he reached for her and drew her in his arms, hugging her tightly against him, his clothes and skin reeking of smoke.

She snaked her arms around his neck and leaned into him, giving him the comfort he so desperately sought, while allowing herself to draw solace from him.

Chapter Fifteen

"*This* is how you're going to put the company back together?"

Ethan and Jillian immediately jumped back from each other. "Father," he said, caught off guard not only by his father's presence, but by the anger in his voice. "I thought you were at home resting."

"Resting? Not when there's work to be done." He gave Ethan and Jillian a derisive sneer. "And it looks like I'm the only person who cares about Vincent and Son going up in flames."

Ethan could only stand there and stare at his father. Gone was the defeated man he'd sent home a couple hours before. The man who had been so contrite for coldly kicking his son out of the family business had returned. The only indication that Harold Vincent had been affected by the fire was the bandage covering the burn on his neck. He had even shaved and was dressed in one of his finer suits. If anything his father seemed more determined, more focused than ever. And more disapproving than ever.

It was painfully apparent nothing had changed.

"This isn't what it looks like," Ethan started.

"I think it's precisely what it looks like. The company is on the brink of ruin and here you are, playing kissy face with some tart you picked up off the street."

"Father—"

"I am *not* a tart," Jillian said, her shoulders squaring indignantly.

Harold harrumphed in response.

"*Father*," Ethan said, more forcefully this time, struggling to keep his temper in check. His strained relationship with Harold wasn't the issue—rebuilding the company was. "This is Jillian Sanders. As in Sanders Shipping."

"Ah, I see you took my advice," Harold gave Jillian a rather deprecating visual once over. "Although it's a little late for it now, don't you think?"

"What advice?" Jillian asked.

"Never mind," Ethan interjected quickly. Blast his father for bringing up that spying business now. They didn't need to bicker over something that never happened, and never would happen. Frantic to keep his father from saying anything else incriminating—or just plain stupid—Ethan spoke. "I found something quite peculiar this morning." He motioned for Harold to follow him as he walked near the edge of the dock, hoping the distraction would be successful.

He breathed a sigh of relief when both Jillian and Harold complied.

Ethan hunkered down and pointed to the drops on the wooden dock planks. "It's some type of oil. Or fuel."

"Fuel?" With some effort, Harold knelt down next to his son. "We don't transport fuel. Or oil, for that matter."

"That's what makes it so odd." Ethan rose, offering to help his father up, who immediately waved him off. "I also found this," Ethan continued, ignoring his father's refusal of his help. He retrieved the bloodied handkerchief from his pocket.

Jillian gasped.

Both men turned and looked at her. The color had drained from her face, her gaze riveted on the handkerchief.

"Jillian?" Ethan said, coming to her. "Are you all right?"

"Y-yes," she said, stopping her scrutiny of the handkerchief. Her expression immediately became as blank as an unspoiled canvas. "I'm fine. Why?"

"You seemed really surprised to see this." He held the handkerchief out in front of him.

"Yes. *Very* surprised." Harold looked at her pointedly. "Do you know who this belongs to?"

Her eyes grew wide. "No. How would I know where that handkerchief came from?"

Harold took the cloth from Ethan's grasp and examined the fabric closely. "There are some initials on here."

"RS," Ethan said. "I noticed them earlier."

"RS," Harold glanced at Jillian with narrowed eyes. "Isn't your brother named Roland Sanders?"

"Yes, but that doesn't mean that belongs to him. I'm sure there are a lot of people in San Francisco that have those initials."

"Who would also have business on the docks? Who would have a vested interest in seeing my company fail?"

Jillian lifted her chin. "Mr. Vincent, I don't like what you're implying."

Harold smirked. "The evidence speaks for itself, Miss Sanders. Fuel oil residue. A bloody handkerchief with your brother's initials on it.

My two best ships bursting into flame for no apparent reason."

"Mr. Vincent!" her voice rose several octaves. "My brother would never do anything to harm your ships, or your company. He has no reason to."

"Oh, I think he has every reason to. I'm sure he would like nothing better than to put Vincent and Son out of business. But I won't let him—that I can guarantee you. I'll make sure he pays for his crimes—"

"Roland did not commit any crime!"

"Father, please!" Ethan stood between the two of them, one almost bursting with rage, the other nearly bursting with indignation. He took the handkerchief from his father's hand and faced Jillian. "Tell me this isn't Roland's," he said quietly, holding it out to Jillian. "Tell me this doesn't belong to your brother, and we'll drop the subject entirely."

She glanced down at the handkerchief in his hand. Her bottom lip moved slightly. But when she looked at him her eyes were steady and clear. "No. That is not Roland's."

Ethan sucked in a deep breath. She was lying. He could tell. He could also tell she was very, very good at it. If it hadn't been for her quivering lip and miniscule hesitation he would have believed her.

He felt as if an anchor had been dropped on him, knocking his breath away. All his illusions of her were shattered, lying in pieces at his feet. She was a liar.

Suddenly he realized who the man was he'd seen prowling about the docks last night, the one with the bruised and swollen face. He had no doubt now that man was Roland Sanders. Her brother had most likely sabotaged the company ships, yet still she had the gall to pretend to sympathize with him, to offer him comfort . . .

To hold him as if she never wanted to let go.

"Ethan?" she looked at him expectantly, a frown forming on those lips he had thought of so many times.

"I have to go." He turned on his heel. "We should both leave, Father."

"I'm not going any—"

"Now!"

Shock registered on Harold's face, but he didn't protest. Without another sound he turned and followed his son.

"Ethan, wait . . ." Jillian called out.

But he didn't turn around. He couldn't bear to look at her. Not without his heart crumbling into tiny pieces.

* * *

From behind several oak barrels stacked on the Vincent docks, Dell watched the thin streams of smoke rising from the sea with smug satisfaction. It was done. The destruction of Vincent's ships would set Harold back years, and he doubted the company could ever be restored to its former glory. Even better, he could see Harold and Ethan facing each other, another woman standing by Ethan's side. Harold looked angry enough to explode, while his son looked guilty and defensive. Dell smiled. Tearing the Vincent family apart was an added bonus.

Well done, Dell. Well done.

Disguising himself as an old sailor and hiring a pathetic, desperate man to do the actual dirty work was a stroke of genius. The sabotage would never be traced back to Dell. Now all he had to do was slip back to the cave, collect his money, and hightail it out of San Francisco. He'd head south, maybe even as far as New Mexico Territory. There he would set up a new identity, a new life.

And it would all be paid for with Harold Vincent's money.

Chapter Sixteen

Jillian's blood ran as cold as the deepest, darkest depths of the ocean. She watched Ethan and his father stalk away from her, and she could almost physically sense their fury.

Outside she may have appeared calm, but she was quaking inside. And hurting. And angry.

She hadn't wanted to lie to Ethan. But what other choice did she have? The handkerchief was definitely Roland's. Despite the blood stains she instantly recognized the monogram. She should have—she had given him the handkerchief as a birthday gift two years ago.

Her arms stiff at her sides, she clenched her

fists. What kind of trouble had her brother gotten himself into this time?

Suddenly the anger was replaced by worry as she realized the blood had been real. Fear clutched at her as she grabbed her skirts and raced back to the hotel. Horrible thoughts ran through her mind. What if he was hurt and abandoned somewhere? What if he was unconscious? What if he was—"

Stop it! She shut her mind off as she ran through the hotel lobby and up the stairs to Roland's room. She pounded on his door, indifferent to the early hour. "Roland! Roland! Are you in there?"

She banged her fist on the door several more times. Muted shouts of "Shut up" and "Pipe down" came through the doors of the other hotel rooms. But Jillian didn't care. All she could think about was her poor baby brother, all alone, possibly dying—

"For pity's sake, Jilly, keep it down! I'm nursing a wallop of a headache here."

She didn't know whether to cry with relief or smack him with fury. There, standing in the doorway, sporting a swollen black-and-blue eye and a crusted-over lip, was her baby brother. Safe and partially sound.

Until she killed him, that is.

"Roland!" Charging into the room, she shoved him out of the way and slammed the door behind her. "Don't ever, ever, *ever*, do that to me again."

"Do what?" He walked over to the bed and laid down on it.

"Scare me like that."

"Scare you like what? You're talking in circles, Jilly."

"Then let me shed some light on the conversation." She stomped over to the window and lifted up the shade. Bright morning sunlight streamed into the window and directly into Roland's eyes.

"Crikey, Jillian, what did you do that for?" he winced as he shielded his eyes. "Put down the bloody shade!"

"I will—when you tell me what you were doing at the Vincent docks last night."

He froze, his hand still hovering over his forehead, his head lifted off the pillow. "The docks? I wasn't at any docks last night."

"Then where were you?"

"Well, *Mother*," he said in a voice dripping with derision, "if you must know, I was out gambling."

"Where?"

"Near the mining camps. There's always a fellow or two up for a game of cards."

Jillian dropped the shade, then lit the oil lamp on the small bedside table. She inspected his injuries. "I take it you lost?"

He sank back into the bed and shut his good eye. "You take it correctly."

"So you decided to burn up a couple of ships to make you feel better?"

He hesitated for a moment. "I didn't touch the Vincent ships."

She lifted one suspicious brow. "How did you know they belonged to Vincent?"

He paused again. "Everyone knows by now," he said finally, not looking at her directly. "You can't keep something like that a secret, Jilly."

She sat down on the side of the bed next to him and sighed, her soul heavy within her. "I suppose not."

He sat up straight, apparently oblivious to the pain of his injuries. His eyes implored her. "Jilly, you've got to believe me. I didn't set fire to those ships."

"Then what was your handkerchief doing on their docks?"

Her question made him pause for a third time. "I-I don't know," he said haltingly. "Maybe . . . maybe I took a stroll down there a few days back and dropped it."

"You, strolling on the Vincent docks? You don't even stroll on *our* docks! And why would there be so much blood on the handkerchief?"

He reached for her hand and clasped it in both of his, the gesture almost desperate. "Jilly, please. I know I've done some despicable things, and I know I can be a cad, but I'm telling you the truth. I had nothing to do with the fire."

She searched his eyes, the same shade of blue as her own. The same color their mother's had been, although Jillian didn't really remember her. All her knowledge of her mother came from the tales her father had told. She had died at such a young age. It had been the three of them since then. No matter what, they always stood by each other.

And she would stand by him now. Regardless of whatever doubts were niggling at her. "I believe you," she told him, squeezing his hand.

Visibly relieved, he leaned until his forehead touched her knuckles. "Thank you, thank you."

"But Roland, while I may believe you, the Vincents aren't going to." She thought back to the accusation in Harold's eyes, and the coldness in Ethan's when she had lied to him. A hard knot formed in the pit of her belly. He hadn't believed her. That much was obvious.

"We'll just have to tell them I didn't do it, Jilly. You're friendly with Ethan Vincent, aren't you?"

"How did you know that?"

"You can't have many secrets in this town." His eyes took on an odd, faraway look. He shook his head hard before bringing his attention back to her. "Surely you can convince him I'm innocent?"

"No," she said, the knot in her stomach doubling up on itself. "I can't. I doubt Ethan Vincent will have anything to do with me ever again."

Roland frowned. "I'm sorry," he said.

"I think you actually mean that."

"I do, Jilly. I do want you to be happy." He released her hand and averted his gaze.

"You have a funny way of showing it."

Sadness seeped into his expression. "I know." He stood up. "I have to go."

"Roland, I don't think this is the time to take off right now."

He grabbed his hat and placed it on his head. "I'll be back later," he said. Then as an afterthought he leaned over and kissed her on the cheek. "Believe it or not I do love you, sis." Then he fled from the room.

"I love you . . . too," she said, her voice fading as he shut the door behind him.

She put her fingertips to her temples and began to rub. Her life was becoming one big lie.

She perpetuated the lie about who really ran Sanders Shipping. She lied to herself about her feelings for Ethan. And she lied to the man she'd grown to care about more than anyone else.

"To protect the family," she whispered aloud. "I had to do it to protect the family."

But her mantra rang hollow, even to her.

Chapter Seventeen

Dell walked into his cave, glancing at the pile of smoldering ashes just outside the entrance. He'd burned the sailor clothes soon after he'd buried John Palmer's body. He wouldn't leave a trace of evidence behind.

He loaded his bags on Palmer's horse, then hoisted himself into the saddle. He tucked a piece of chewing tobacco between his lower lip and gum, smiling as he did. His brand new, very *rich* life was awaiting him.

Within an hour he was outside San Francisco, heading south toward the California border. He'd decided to go to Mexico now that the war was over. Dusk was approaching as he traveled down a dusty, abandoned road. Soon he would stop to camp for the night.

Suddenly out of nowhere came the sound of a gunshot. Dell felt a sharp streak of air whiz past his left ear. Before he realized what happened, hoof beats thundered behind him. He glanced over his shoulder. Two men with handkerchiefs covering their faces quickly pulled their horses up beside him. One held a gun point-blank at Dell's chest.

"You'll be stoppin' now," the man shouted.

Dell reached for his holster instead, and got a bullet in the hand for his effort.

"Like I was sayin', you'll be stoppin' now."

Pain pierced Dell's hand as he pulled the horse to a stop. Warm blood ran down and over his wrist. He moved to touch his holster again.

"You reach for your gun one more time and that'll be the last thing you ever do. Now raise your hands up high, both of 'em."

Anger mixed with fear crashed inside Dell, but he did as he was told. Helplessly he watched as the other man lifted the saddlebags off Palmer's horse. Useless fury raged inside him. These darn men were stealing everything he had. And there was nothing he could do about it.

"We'll be takin' these," the taller man said, snickering as he took the bags away.

The man with the gun grabbed the reins of Dell's horse. "We'll also be takin' your horse." He kicked Dell hard in the side, knocking him off the animal. Dell hit the ground with a thud, his cheek slamming against the pebbled, dusty road.

With a tilt of his head, the thief gestured to the other man. "Make it so he don't follow us."

Still clutching his side, his face, head and hand throbbing with pain, Dell looked up at the man above him. The robber raised the butt of his shotgun up in the air. Dell's eyes grew wide. The gun connected with the center of his forehead.

Stars exploded behind his eyes. The fading sounds of the robbers laughing and horses galloping away in the distance reached Dell's ears. Soon everything went black.

"Where is your brother, Ms. Sanders?"

Jillian's heart leaped to her throat. Standing in the doorway of the Sanders Shipping office was a furious looking Harold Vincent. He was accompanied by a stern man she'd never seen before.

"This is no time for stalling." Harold barged into the room. "Where is Roland Sanders?"

"I-I don't know," Jillian replied, rising from her seat behind the desk. She was telling the truth. She hadn't seen Roland since early that morning, even though he'd said he wouldn't be gone long.

"You're lying!" Harold pounded his fist on the desk, sending a few pieces of paper fluttering to the floor. "Stop protecting him."

Jillian flinched, but quickly regained her composure. She squared her shoulders. "I'm not lying. And I'm not protecting him."

"Sheriff Cooper," Harold said to the other man. "I demand you take this woman into custody. Maybe a night in a jail cell will jog her memory!"

"Now hold on a minute, Harold," Cooper said calmly, removing his weather-beaten cowboy hat. "I can't just go around arresting people for no good reason."

"No good reason? She's harboring a fugitive from justice."

"I'm not harboring anyone," she protested.

"Jillian."

She spun around to see Ethan walking into the room. His expression was guarded, his gray eyes filled with an unusual emotion. Disappointment, she soon realized, causing her spirits to sink low.

He moved to stand in front of her. "Don't make this difficult, Jillian. Just tell them where Roland is."

Suddenly she felt like a mouse being chased into a corner. She gave each of the men a long, hard look. "I haven't seen Roland since this morning. How many times must I say it?"

"And why should we believe you?" Harold sneered. "You lied to us about the handkerchief."

"I did not—"

"Jillian, please," Ethan interjected. He lowered his voice. "I know the handkerchief is Roland's."

She took a deep breath. "All right," she admitted reluctantly. To continue to lie would make a bad situation even worse. "The handkerchief is Roland's." She stepped toward Ethan, looking into his eyes. "You have to understand, I was only trying to protect him."

"Just as I suspected," Harold said.

Jillian ignored him. "But I don't have to protect him anymore. He told me this morning he didn't destroy your ships."

"And you believe him?"

"He's my brother, of course I believe him."

"A brother who's nothing more than a ne'er-do-well," Harold said, stepping between her and Ethan. "I've been doing some checking on your family and on your company. There are some strange goings-on here. Such as how a man who's been spied gambling and drinking at mining camps on a regular basis is able to run a profitable shipping business?"

She rubbed her lips together. Although it was relatively cool in the office, she could feel perspiration beading on her forehead. "He's a man of many talents," she said weakly.

Harold smugly crossed his arms and rested them over his rotund belly. "Still, even such a talented man should visit his docks every once in a while. But upon inquiring of your crews and workers, they say they see very little of the owner."

"He—he prefers to run things from afar. Roland's, ah, never been hands-on with the business."

"Apparently he was *very* hands-on with my ships last night."

"I told you he didn't do it! I'll admit Roland's ways are a little . . . unusual. But my brother would never do something as horrible—and criminal—as deliberately sabotaging your company. Besides, what motive would he have?"

"Putting Vincent and Son out of business. That's all the motive he needs."

Jillian shook her head. *If they only knew how little he cared about Vincent & Son. Or Sanders Shipping for that matter.*

"If this is another attempt at stonewalling us—"

"Father, please." Ethan held up his hand, and

nudged Harold out of the way. "Badgering Jilly isn't getting us anywhere." He looked at her, his eyes softening for the first time since they'd embraced on the dock earlier that morning. It surprised her, just as his next words did. "We need to talk. In private," he added, casting Harold a pointed look.

"Ethan, I don't think that's a good idea," Harold stated.

"I do." Sheriff Cooper placed his hat back on his head and led Harold to the door. "Maybe Ethan can get to the bottom of this."

With a sputter of protests, Harold exited the room with the sheriff, leaving Ethan and Jillian alone.

To her surprise, Ethan grabbed her hand. "I think I understand what's going on," he said quietly.

"You do?"

"Yes. You've been lying to me, to my father, even to the sheriff. And I believe I know why." He paused, rubbing his thumb against her hand. "You can trust me with the truth, Jilly. It's the only thing that's going to save your brother . . . and you."

Ethan watched as Jillian extricated her hand from his, then sank down into the chair. Her shoulders slumped, her expression haggard, she looked exhausted. The anger and resentment he'd felt for her moments ago immediately evaporated. If what he suspected was true, she'd been carrying a very big burden, and carrying it alone. His heart squeezed in his chest as she didn't say anything, didn't even look at him. She simply exhaled a defeated sigh.

He went and knelt down before her. "Jilly, talk to me, please. Tell me what all this is about?"

She looked up at him, tears shining in her eyes. "You were right about me," she said, her chin quivering. "I am a liar. I've been lying to you . . . to everyone, for a long time. You should hate me."

"I don't hate you."

"Why are you being so nice?"

"Because I choose to believe you must have a good reason for the deception." He wiped away the moisture that slipped down her cheek. "And I care about you, Jillian Sanders. When are you going to accept that?"

A trembling smile broke through her sadness. "I guess I just don't understand why. I've been pushing you away practically since the day we met."

"So why don't you tell me why you're doing it?"

"Because I had to protect the company. And my family. What little there is left of it, that is."

Ethan stood and pulled up an empty chair and sat down, waiting for her to explain.

"My father died a few months ago, but you already knew that. Now it's just Roland and me."

"What about your mother?"

"She died in childbirth. With Roland."

"I'm so sorry."

She looked at him. "I'm not telling you this to earn your pity," she said, an edge creeping into her voice. "That's the last thing I want."

"And that's the last thing you're going to get."

His words seemed to reassure her. She continued talking. "My father built his shipping business from the ground up. He was the son of an exiled convict from England. He made Sanders Shipping the biggest shipping business in Australia. It was his dream to expand to California. But he died before he could do it himself. So he relied on Roland, and on me. He left Roland in charge of running the new arm of the company while his business partner took care of things back in Sydney."

"Roland's not interested in running a business?"

She nodded. "He never has been. But I couldn't let Father's dream fail. I just couldn't do that."

"So you've been doing it yourself." Ethan leaned forward. "And you protected your brother at the same time by working behind the scenes."

"I didn't want anyone to find out. How would it look to everyone if they knew a woman was in charge of Sanders Shipping? Especially to people like your father? No one would take us seriously. So I perpetuated the illusion that Roland was the boss. With the help of a very discreet captain, I kept the company afloat, so to speak.

"Then I learned your family owned Vincent and Son, our chief rival. And even though I liked you, even though I wanted to, I couldn't get close to you. The risk of you finding out my secret was too great."

He reached for her hand. "I don't understand why you're still protecting Roland, Jilly. He's caused you nothing but hardship."

"He's my brother, Ethan. I love him. And despite all his faults, deep down he's a good person. I know that in my heart."

"Jilly, do you really think he's innocent this time? I saw him on our docks last night, but I didn't realize it was him until I found the handkerchief. He had been beaten, that much was obvious."

He heard her suck in a breath. "Did he tell you what he was doing there?"

"He claimed he was lost. But he had been talking with an old sailor, one who was not in our employ. The man disappeared as soon as I approached them."

"Maybe Roland was talking to one of your crew?"

"I don't think so. He acted as if the man were a stranger. Jilly, I hate to say this, but all the evidence points to him. He was at the docks before the fire occurred. He was with a suspicious person. His handkerchief was found near the edge of the dock, where we found drops of fuel."

"Was there fuel on his handkerchief?"

Ethan leaned back. "No."

"Then you really don't have anything but conjecture."

He released her hand, then ran his fingers through his hair. "What happened to Roland last night? Why was he beaten? And where is he now?"

"I—I don't know."

"Look at me, Jilly." He gazed at her intently. "Do you really think he's innocent?"

"Yes," she whispered, hugging her arms around her body as if the room had suddenly turned chilly. "I have to."

Yet he could see the doubt creeping in to her eyes. Her loyalty was admirable, if misplaced.

"Ethan, I know I don't have the right to ask . . ." she stared down at her hands, which were clasped so tightly in her lap the knuckles had turned white. "But . . . could you please not say anything about what I just told you?"

"About who's running your company? No, your secret is safe with me." He paused, knowing what he was about to say next would upset her. "But we have to find Roland."

"Ethan—"

"If he's innocent like you say, then I promise he'll have a chance to clear himself. But Jilly, even you have to admit, his disappearing like this doesn't look good."

"I know." Tentatively, she reached for his hand. "Thank you, Ethan."

He didn't reply, just savored the feel of her soft skin against his. There was so much more that needed to be said, but this wasn't the time. There was so much more between them, but neither of them could hope for a future together, not right now.

He wondered if they ever could.

Chapter Eighteen

Roland paced back and forth, fingering the wad of bills in his pocket. Money he'd gotten from setting the Vincent ships on fire. Money he needed to pay off his gambling debt.

He was at an abandoned claim, a couple of rusty, shallow sifting pans the only remnants of the former occupant of the rocky patch of land. Every bone in his body ached. His swollen face throbbed with pain. But this time his troubles didn't just affect him. They wholly affected Jilly as well.

How could he fix this? He had to pay his debt, or the bloke that had beaten him within an inch of his life before would finish off the job. At the moment, that didn't seem like such a bad idea.

However, where would that leave Jilly? Much better off, he thought miserably. Her life would be a lot easier without him around.

But what if his deeds had repercussions beyond him? For the first time he forced himself to think about the future, and about someone other than himself. If Boxer didn't receive his money, without a doubt he'd send his thugs after Jilly.

The thought made him sick.

He lowered himself to the ground and stared at the vast stretch of land before him, as if it held the answers he needed. It didn't.

On impulse he reached in the inside pocket of his jacket and pulled out a folded, worn envelope. Slowly he laid it flat against his knee and read the name on the front. His name, written in wobbly script by his ailing father.

Roland stared at the envelope. It was still sealed. Although his father's solicitor had given it to him right after the reading of the will, Roland hadn't wanted to open it. He could guess what was inside. A list of instructions on how to run the company. Or a list of Roland's faults—his father never seemed to tire of that subject. Whatever he had written, Roland knew it couldn't be good. Nothing about his relationship with his father had ever been good.

Still, he'd carried the letter around with him. He didn't know why. It's not as if he'd thought about it very much. But for some reason he had to have it with him. And now, looking at the crooked letters formed by a gravely ill man, sorrow suddenly permeated him. His hand shaking, he slid his finger beneath the frayed seal, then withdrew the letter from the inside.

Roland,

A man ponders much when facing the end of his life. He thinks back on his accomplishments and his failures. His triumphs. And his regrets. Of those I have many. But my biggest regret of all is how I have failed you.

The only thing I wanted in life was to be a successful person. To be more than my father was. More than the son of an exiled criminal. As much as I wanted that, I wanted more for my son. Even before you were born, I pictured us running my company together, side by side, taking on Australia, and eventually the world.

But fate dealt a cruel blow when your mother died. I'll admit now what I was too proud, and too ashamed, to admit then. I blamed you for your mother's death. I placed a heavy burden on you before you were even a day old. And although I told myself I kept those dark feelings buried deep inside, I know you must have felt them.

Then all too soon you grew up. You became a lad full of life. Always smiling, always laughing, never serious. Solemnity, unfortunately, is your sister's burden to bear. And I suppose I resented you for that too, for your love of life. Because how dare you enjoy living when my Shannon was gone.

In time it was much easier to find fault in you than to accept fault in my feelings. As I spent more time with Jillian, I pushed you away. I was cruel, and took out my anger on you. For that I am deeply sorry, as I am sorry I will not be able to tell you these things to your face. A letter is a very poor substitute for what I should have done a long time ago—told you how much I loved you. How much I believe in you. How much you deserve to lead Sanders Shipping into the future.

Your sister can help you learn about the company. I know it won't take you long to get your wits about you, you've always been a bright lad. But don't let her boss you around or take over, as she has a tendency to do. This is your company, son. Your legacy.

Your most undeserving father,

James Sanders

Roland folded up the letter and let out a shuddering sigh. Tears rolled down his cheeks, and he wiped them quickly with the back of his sleeve. Anger warred with sadness as he thought about his father's letter. Why didn't he tell him all this when he was alive? Did he really think a single page of words would make years of heartache, years of feeling second-rate, vanish instantly?

He took a deep breath and stood up. *I believe in you.* The sentiment was chipping away at him. His father had believed in him. Jilly believed in him now.

All he needed to do was believe in himself.

Chapter Nineteen

They could hear Ethan's father grumbling outside the office door. Ethan offered Jillian a look of encouragement as he squeezed her hand.

"I've waited long enough!" Harold blustered as he flung open the door. It banged against the wall behind it. He marched into the room, Sheriff Cooper close on his heels. He headed straight for Jillian.

"If you don't tell me where your brother is this instant you'll live to regret it."

Ethan heard Jillian gasp at the threat. He released her hand and sprang up from the chair. "Father," he warned, his voice low and menacing. "That is enough."

Harold glared at him. “First you refuse to seek out information about their company, now you’re siding with her against me.”

“I’m not siding against you,” Ethan started, exasperated they were going down this well-worn road again.

“You wanted him to spy on me?” Jillian quickly rose from her seat.

“Not that it mattered,” Harold muttered. “Apparently he would rather disregard his family.”

“I’m not disregarding anyone!” Ethan insisted. “What you wanted me to do was wrong, Father. Very wrong. I’m sure Mother would agree.”

“You leave your Mother out of this,” Harold snapped. “Women have no place in the business world.”

“Jillian.”

They all turned around to see who had spoken. Complete silence fell as Roland Sanders entered it, looking more battered than he had the night before. His one good eye narrowed as he approached Harold.

“It’s over,” he said, then looked at Ethan and the sheriff. “Leave Jillian alone.” He finally met his sister’s eyes, and his expression softened. “I’m here to turn myself in.”

* * *

"Are you comfortable?" Jillian asked.

Roland let out flat chuckle. "About as comfortable as a man can be in a jail cell."

She sighed, blinking back the tears that threatened to fall. Her brother's injuries seemed even more severe behind the iron bars of the tiny room. She watched as he walked to the warped cot on the left side of the cell and lay down gingerly on the tattered and stained wool blanket.

He had confessed everything to the sheriff, Harold, and Ethan shortly after they'd arrived at Cooper's office. Jillian had listened with shock and disbelief as Roland had explained being approached by the sailor who offered him money to torch Vincent's ships, and how he had been desperate enough to accept it. He also told about his gambling debts, which had led to his beating the night before.

His confessions had also revealed who had been truly running Sanders Shipping all along.

"I've gotten both of us in trouble, haven't I?" Roland asked.

"I don't know." She sat down in the uncomfortable wooden chair right outside the cell and stared at her lap. The sheriff had kindly brought it to her after the Vincents' departure. He seemed like a fair and just man, but it didn't matter. Roland was guilty. The only thing left was to determine his punishment. That, and to figure out her future.

"I'm sorry, Jilly." Roland mumbled weakly from his prone position on the cot. "I truly am sorry. I let you down again. Just like I always let Father down."

She looked at him. He was bruised, bloody, and way too pale and thin. "Why, Roland? How did all this happen? How could you let things go so far?"

He continued to stare up at the ceiling. "I don't know. I guess I was born a loser."

"Oh no. Don't you dare blame the circumstances of your birth for the bad choices you made."

He didn't say anything.

Standing up, she paced in front of the bars. "I wonder where Sheriff Cooper is. I told him to bring you back a meal from the hotel. You'll need to keep your strength up."

He sat up, and winced as he got up from the cot. He pulled something from his pants pocket. "Here," he said, passing the folded paper to her between two of the bars.

She took it from his fingers. "What is it?"

"Just read it."

Unfolding the paper, she immediately recognized her father's handwriting. A few sentences into the letter, a teardrop fell from her cheek and onto the paper.

She thought back to the reading of the will, to when the lawyer had named Roland the head of Sanders Shipping. They both had been shocked. And in all truth, she had been jealous. While Roland had piddled and whiled away his life, she had been by her father's side, learning the business, educating herself on how to manage a company. She had eventually assumed the only reason her father had put Roland in charge was because as a woman she simply couldn't run the company outright. Now she realized she was wrong.

When she finished reading, she carefully folded the letter. "I didn't know he'd felt that way about Mother, Roland," she said. "He never said anything to me."

"Nor to me." He leaned wearily against the bars, pressing his forehead to the cold metal. "But I knew. Somehow, deep down, I knew."

She stood up and touched his hand. "But he also told you he was sorry. And that he believed in you. It's all in the letter."

"But why couldn't he have told me while he was alive?" Roland pounded his head once against the bar. His shoulders slumped. "Perhaps it wouldn't have made a difference."

"Perhaps it would have." And Jillian believed it. Her heart swelled with sorrow and pity for her brother. Even after everything, she still loved him. She also admired his courage, and this new-found sense of responsibility. Unfortunately it had come at so high a cost.

"The gambling has to stop," she said.

He looked at her, and for a split second a mischievous glint alighted in his eye. "It would be difficult to continue under these circumstances, don't you think?"

"You won't be in here forever."

"If Vincent has his way I'll rot behind these bars." He looked at her, his Adam's apple bobbing up and down. "But if I ever do get out of here Jilly, I promise you I'll change. I won't let you down. Not anymore."

She believed him. The sincerity in his eyes, in the tone of his voice. And her heart ached, because she wasn't sure he'd ever have a second chance. But she couldn't let him know her doubts. She forced herself to smile in encouragement. "Thank you, Roland. That means so much. But don't do it for me. Do it for yourself."

"I will, Jilly. Believe me, I will."

Chapter Twenty

"He should hang for what he's done."

Ethan brought his fingers to the bridge of his nose and closed his eyes. "He didn't kill anyone, Father."

"He certainly could have. What if there had been a sentry on one of the ships? Or a crew member down below Sanders didn't know about?" Harold continued to stomp back and forth in front of his desk at the Vincent and Son office. "The man must pay."

"I'm fairly sure he already has," Ethan mumbled, remembering the haunted look on Roland's face, not to mention the complete devastation on Jillian's. He frowned as he thought of what her brother's treachery had cost his family's company—and her.

"I don't trust Cooper," Harold continued, his face turning an explosive shade of red. "Since that debacle with Watkins—"

"That wasn't Sheriff Cooper's fault. Watkins was well out of town limits when he escaped his escort."

"Well, I will make sure that Sanders has no chance to escape. By the time I'm through with him he'll wish he'd stayed in Australia!"

"Tea, dear?"

Both men turned to see Bessie standing in the doorway, a false smile pasted on her lips. To Ethan she seemed a little pale, and her gray eyes hinted at a mood other than her usual jovial one. Without waiting for either of them to answer she walked into the room, set the silver tray down on a small table near the fireplace, and then stood in place.

Harold's expression softened slightly, as it often did when he was around his wife. "Bessie, Ethan and I were just discussing some very important business. If you'll excuse us—"

"No, I don't believe I will." She clasped her small hands together and looked directly at her husband. "And I know exactly what kind of business you're discussing. I'm sure the whole of San Francisco also knows by now."

Harold moved over to her and placed his hand on her shoulder, then started to guide her in the direction of the doorway. But Bessie stood her ground. "You will not dismiss me, Harold. Not this time."

"Bessie, I must insist—"

"Harold, that is part of your problem. You insist on everything. And if you're not insisting, you're demanding or yelling or swearing . . . and I won't put up with it any further."

Apparently taken aback, Harold grimaced. "You don't know what you're talking about," he said, stalking back to his desk. He began flipping through the papers littered all over the surface of it. "What do you know about my business dealings anyway?"

"I know that they've changed you, darling." Her voice was soft as she spoke, her eyes kind, yet determined. She went to her husband and touched his face. "You used to be such a sweet man, Harold."

Clearly Bessie was having an effect on her husband, because their gazes were locked and he was actually listening to her. "I've stood by for years, watching you struggle to build this company. I know it's taken hard work and perseverance, and I know at times you've had to be rough with others to get results." She cupped his cheek in her hand. "But now you've become a tyrant, not only at work, but at home as well. You even tried to recruit your son as a spy, just so you could get ahead of your competition."

Harold's brow lifted. "You know about that?"

"I know more than you think. I've remained silent up until now, but I won't anymore. I won't watch you ruin your relationship with your son. Or with me."

He slumped into the chair behind his desk, and looked at Ethan. "Is what she's saying true?"

Ethan nodded, bolstered by his mother's own bravery. "That you've become a tyrant? Yes."

Harold paused. He stared down at his desktop for a moment. "And what about our relationship? Is it . . ."

"Ruined?" Ethan rose from his chair and went to his father. "I love you, Father. That will never change. And I used to respect you. But now . . . I don't know."

Harold leaned back in his chair, his expression solemn. "I never wanted to lose your respect, Ethan. I just wanted my company—our company—to be the best it could be."

"I realize that. But taking revenge on Roland

Sanders isn't going to solve anything. His company has been damaged as much as ours. Maybe more so."

Harold looked from Ethan to Bessie, who gave her husband a smile of encouragement. Then he looked back at Ethan, his expression softening. "When did you become so wise?"

"I had a great teacher," Ethan said, sitting down. "Once upon a time."

Harold sighed, and Bessie walked over to him and put her hand on his shoulder. He covered it with his own and looked up at her. They exchanged a tender glance filled with unspoken meaning. Then he looked back at Ethan. "I don't suppose you have any ideas as to what we should do next," he said.

Ethan leaned back in his chair and folded his hands together. A plan had occurred to him while they were at Cooper's office, but his father had been too steeped in his own rants of revenge that he hadn't wanted to listen to anything. But now was Ethan's chance. "Actually, I do," he said, his mouth forming a large smile. "I think I have a solution that will work out for all of us."

Jillian stared out the window of Sheriff Cooper's office. The hustle and bustle of the afternoon was dying down as dusk was settling over the town. Men, women, and children strolled down the boardwalk, rode in fancy carriages or in the backs of wagons. Even through the glass she could hear the occasional joyful shout or gleeful tinkling of laughter. And why shouldn't they all be happy, she thought bitterly. Their lives weren't falling apart.

Just hers and Roland's.

"You don't have to stay here, Ms. Sanders," Sheriff Cooper said. "Nothing's going to happen to your brother."

Turning around, she peered inside the jail cell. Her brother was lying on the cot, one arm flung across his chest, which rose and fell softly. He had finally succumbed to sleep, and Jillian surmised it wasn't because of some newfound sense of peace. He had literally passed out from exhaustion.

"I can't leave him alone," she said softly. "Not yet." She turned and faced the window again, looking out into the dusty town street but not seeing anything. Her mind was spinning with confusion. What would happen to Roland? How could Sanders Shipping rebound from such a scandal? Should she try to salvage any part of the business she could? Or more importantly, would she even be able to?

Blinking back tears, she swallowed. It was over, plain and simple. She would have to return to Sydney. Her brother probably would never return to Australia. She had to resign herself to the possibility she would never see him again.

And what of Ethan? No matter how hard she tried, she couldn't banish him from her thoughts. Or from her heart. She loved him, and she was through lying to herself about it. But that didn't matter either. Even if there were a way she could fix all that was wrong, he probably would never forgive her or Roland for what her brother had done to Vincent and Son.

Sighing, she started to move away from the window when she saw Ethan and Harold Vincent crossing the street. They were heading straight for Cooper's office with determined expressions.

Anxiety pooled in her stomach. She hadn't thought to see them so soon. Before she had crossed the room to stand protectively in front of Roland's cell, the two men barged into the office.

Harold saw her first. She gripped her reticule tightly, ready for another verbal attack. To her deep shock he merely removed his hat and said, "Miss Sanders. We didn't expect to see you here."

"Where else would I be?" she replied, her tone guarded.

"A jailhouse isn't exactly a place for a lady."

"No, it isn't. The only place for a lady, according to you, is trapped at home, ready to do a man's every bidding." The words dripped with sarcasm, but she couldn't help it. She'd had enough of Harold Vincent and his pompous attitude. She may not have much anymore, but she did have her pride.

"Jillian!" Roland, now fully awake, hissed from the cell behind her. "Don't bait the man. That will only make things worse for all of us."

Ethan suddenly stepped forward. "I don't think things can get worse for you, Roland."

Roland frowned. "Thanks for stating the obvious."

"Here's something that might not be so obvious," Ethan said smoothly, unfazed by Roland's barb. "How would you like to permanently leave that cell?"

Chapter Twenty-one

Jillian couldn't believe what she was hearing. Roland appeared to be in complete shock too. Even the stoic Sheriff Cooper was furrowing his brow as Ethan explained his plan for Roland and both shipping companies.

"So let me get this straight," Roland said after Ethan finished speaking. "The only restitution you want from me is *work?* You're suggesting in lieu of jail I come and work for Vincent and Son?"

"That's exactly what I'm suggesting."

Roland folded his arms and rested them against his chest. "There has to be something else. I burned two of your ships."

"We're well aware of that."

Jillian watched their exchange with interest, her initial shock at Ethan's offer wearing off. He seemed to be in complete control, and had a stronger confidence than usual. But even more intriguing was Harold's complete reticence. He seemed perfectly content to let his son handle the situation.

"What I propose is this," Ethan said, moving closer to the bars that separated him from Roland. "You become a member of the *Edwina Columbia*'s crew. Any wages you earn will be applied to the replacement of the destroyed ships."

"That's indentured servitude!"

"I suspect it would be preferable to spending the next several years in jail," Ethan pointed out.

"Roland," Jillian said touching her brother's hand as it gripped one of the bars. "It's a gift. You know it is."

He looked from Jillian to Ethan, then to Harold. "And you're okay with this? Last I heard you wanted my head on a silver platter."

Harold nodded. "My son and I have discussed it. It took a bit of convincing," he acknowledged, causing Ethan to smile slightly, "but I think it will benefit both of us. We get your labor, you pay off your debt." He eyed him directly. "You do know how to sail, don't you?"

Roland's skin took on a hint of greenness.

"Of-of course I do," he said. Jillian could tell he was trying to be stoic. "You don't grow up around ships without learning the ropes."

Jillian suddenly remembered her brother's penchant for seasickness. "Bad puns aside, maybe this isn't such a good idea," she said, but Roland held up his hand to silence her.

"Like you said, Jilly, it's a gift." Then he lowered his voice. "And whatever will happen once I'm out to sea is no less than what I deserve."

Her heart swelled with pride as she regarded Roland. There was a resolute set to his chin, as if he were visibly bolstering his courage. He really seemed serious this time about taking responsibility and paying for his actions. She smiled. Her brother would be all right.

"It's settled, then," Ethan said, extending his hand to shake Roland's. Then he paused and looked back at Cooper. "As long as it's okay with the Sheriff."

"Sounds good to me." He took a set of keys off a hook on the wall and walked over to the cell. "But if he backs out of the deal, Vincent, you feel free to let me know. The jailhouse will be waiting for him."

When Roland was freed, he and Ethan shook hands. "Thank you," Roland said soberly. "I appreciate your faith in me."

"You should thank your sister."

"What?" Jillian exclaimed.

"It was her faith in you, Sanders, that convinced me this arrangement might work. She stood beside you throughout all of this, and that says a lot." He looked at her in that delightfully sweet way of his. "If she believes in you, then I do too."

The door to the sheriff's office suddenly flew open. Three men covered in trail dust came in, dragging a man with them. They unceremoniously dumped him in the middle of the floor.

Jillian gasped. "Is he . . . dead?"

"Naw," the dustiest man said. "He's just knocked out cold."

Everyone, including Sheriff Cooper, gathered around the man to get a better look.

"We found him on our way back to our claims. We didn't know what to do with him, so we just thought we'd let y'all deal with him." The man tipped his hat. "Found him on the side of the road, left fer dead. Looks like he was robbed. Didn't think it were right leavin' him there to be a coyote's dinner. Now if you'll 'scuse us, we be havin' some gold to mine for."

"Jilly," Roland said after the men had left. He crouched down by the body. "I think I know this man."

Ethan knelt beside him, his brow furrowing. "I do too." He looked up at Harold. "It's Watkins."

"It's the sailor who paid me to torch the ships," Roland added.

"Well I'll be," Cooper said, tilting his hat back on his head. "It's Dell alright. Looks like bad luck came round and bit him in the bottom." He walked over to a rusty basin of water and picked up an equally orange colored dipper. Filling it with water, he walked over to Watkins and threw the cold liquid in his face.

"Pfft." Watkins shook his head, spitting out the water. Drops glistened on his beard. "You," he said, making eye contact with Roland. Then he looked at Ethan and his eyes widened. "You!"

"Looks like you've been hand delivered right where you belong," Cooper said, dragging Watkins up by the armpit.

Harold stepped forward. "Where's my money?" he demanded.

Watkins grinned, his teeth brown from tobacco, his eyes filled with black mirth. "Gone. All gone. Stolen." He laughed as if on the verge of hysteria while Cooper locked him up in Roland's former cell.

"And make sure he stays there," Harold boomed.

"Oh don't worry . . . he's not going anywhere." Cooper locked the cell. "I'll guarantee you that."

Satisfied, Harold turned to Roland. "Gather your things, Sanders. The *Edwina Columbia* sets sail tomorrow morning, bright and early. You need to meet the crew, learn the layout of the ship . . ."

Jillian watched as Harold led Roland out of Cooper's office. She couldn't believe this was the same man who had been out for her brother's blood just that morning. So much had changed within the course of the day, all because of Ethan.

All except one thing.

She looked at him. "I don't know how to thank you," she said, her throat tightening. "What you and your father did was beyond generous."

"Not necessarily," Ethan said. "We all benefit, actually. We have an extra crewman, the ships will be rebuilt, and Roland pays off his debt."

Ethan's gray eyes were filled with satisfaction, and even a hint of happiness. Jillian could only imagine what hers conveyed. She could only hope she wasn't betraying a fraction of the pain that seemed to strangle her heart.

She took a deep breath. There was no reason to delay the inevitable. "I guess this is good-bye, then."

He looked genuinely puzzled. "Good-bye? What do you mean?"

"Now that I know Roland's going to be all right, there's no need for me to remain." Tonight she would wish Roland well on his journey, then first thing in the morning she would book passage on the next ship headed for Australia.

"But what about Sanders Shipping?"

Jillian shrugged, averting her gaze, trying to put on a show for Ethan about how unaffected she was by the demise of the company. "Perhaps it's just as well our interests remain in Sydney," she said. "It's less complicated that way. Mr. Holland does a marvelous job managing the company there. I'm sure he will continue to do so."

Ethan moved closer to Jillian. "Then what about us?"

She glanced around the room, suddenly aware of how little distance was between her and Ethan. Somehow Sheriff Cooper had slipped out of the office undetected. They were alone. And Ethan's nearness was almost her undoing. "Please . . . don't make this more difficult."

"But Jillian—"

"Wait. There's something I have to say." She took a deep breath. She would tell him how she truly felt, she owed him that honesty. "I will miss you, Ethan Vincent. I'll think about you every minute I'm gone, every second we're apart. And if circumstances were different . . ." Her voice choked and she turned away. She couldn't finish, couldn't think about what might have been. It hurt too much.

"Sweetheart." His voice was soft, a caress on the back of her neck as he placed his hands on her shoulders. "This isn't good-bye. This is just the beginning."

Slowly she rotated to face him. "The beginning?"

He nodded, his mouth curving into a smile. "There's a second part to our arrangement with Roland, and with you. Our company has suffered a huge loss, as has yours. Instead of two broken companies fighting against each other . . . what do you say about joining them together?"

Her mouth fell open in shock. "Are you serious? Is your *father* serious?"

"One thing about my father, he knows a good business decision when he sees one. And this is a very, very good business decision."

"But how—"

"Why don't we let the lawyers figure all that out." With one smooth motion he swept her up in his arms. "There's just one thing left to do," he said, his voice becoming low and husky.

"And what is that?" she asked, loving the feel

of his muscular arms around her, wrapping her in a warm blanket of strength and security.

"Seal the deal. And I'm not talking about a handshake." He lowered his face toward hers and kissed her gently, at first, then more fervently.

"Wow," he said when they finally broke apart. "We should make deals more often, Jillian Sanders."

"I can't think of having a better partner than you," she said, pressing her cheek against his shoulder. *In business . . . or in love.*

Chapter Twenty-two

Jillian walked into the new offices of Vincent & Sanders Shipping, a letter in her hand. "Ethan!" she called as she went over to his desk. "I got another letter from Roland!"

"Where is he now?" Ethan asked, not looking up.

"China," she said excitedly. "He also sent me this." She flipped open a delicate silk fan. Ornate flowers painted in vibrant colors decorated the stiffened fabric.

"That's lovely, Jillian."

"Hmmph," she said, moving behind his chair. "You haven't even looked at it." She noticed the sketch laid out in front of him and realized what had captivated his attention. “Is that the new ship?”

“Yes,” he said, pointing to the drawing. “The next great vessel in the Vincent/Sanders fleet.”

“Very impressive.”

“I’m glad you think so.”

She studied the drawing with pride. For the past year everyone had been working hard to restore the new company to the former glory of its parent companies. Harold handled the commercial end of the business, allowing Ethan to do what he loved to do—design the ships and oversee their construction. And once Harold had realized what a keen mind Jillian possessed, he put her in charge of the books. The arrangement pleased her—she was relieved not to shoulder all the responsibility anymore, and she was happy to have a major hand in the running of the business.

“Did Roland have anything else to say?” Ethan added another small detail to the sketch with his pencil. “How’s his seasickness?”

“Better,” she said. “Or maybe he’s just getting used to it. He enjoys everything else about the sea and sailing, I guess getting sick for the first day or two doesn’t bother him.”

“Good, good.” After a few more scribbles, he put the pencil down. “What do you think of this?" he asked, pointing to several small marks at the side of the ship's bow.

Jillian leaned in close. "I can't make it out . . . oh wait, now I can. The *Jillian Vincent*." She paused, then stood up straight. The Jillian Vincent? Had he made a mistake? "Don't you mean Sanders?"

Ethan turned in his chair and grabbed her around the waist, pulling her into his lap. "No," he said, kissing the tip of her nose. "I meant Vincent. A fine ship deserves an equally fine name."

"Ethan, I'm not a Vincent."

"But I hope you will be." He held out his hand to her.

She was ready to clasp it until she saw something shiny in the center of his palm. A gold band. Her heart stopped.

"Will you marry me, Jillian?"

She gazed into his wonderful eyes, eyes she had grown to love and cherish, along with the man who possessed them. "Yes," she said breathlessly. "Yes, I'll marry you." Cupping his face in her hands, she brought his mouth to hers, and kissed him soundly.

"So it's a deal?" He grinned.

Jillian nodded, hugging him tightly around his neck. "The best deal I've ever made."

Dear Patron: You are invited to make a brief comment or two, signed or unsigned, after reading this novel. Your comments may help other readers in their book selection. (Positive as well as negative comments are requested.) Thank you.

Mediokra — CEG